NASHVILLE NIGHTMARE

As Diego glanced back, he saw a svelte woman hike up her fashionably ankle-length, split halfway to obscenity skirt, pull out what was clearly a long-barreled knobby weapon of some kind, and fire it at a bald man trying to climb one of the green lampposts dotting the length of the curb. There was a flash of blue light at the muzzle, a beam of stark white light that flared from the muzzle's blue light, and a smoking hole soon appeared in the back of her victim's neck. . . .

Someone pulled out another weapon, this one much more compact and less ostentatious, and burned the woman's hair off.

Praise for Lionel Fenn's *Kent Montana* Books:

"Lightweight and funny farce." —*Kliatt*

"Fans of Craig Shaw Gardner will enjoy these books."
—*Raymond's Reviews*

"Fenn cheerfully demolishes every cliché of every science fiction monster movie you've ever seen."
—Craig Shaw Gardner, bestselling author of *The Cineverse Cycle* and *Batman*

Ace Books by Lionel Fenn

BY THE TIME I GET TO NASHVILLE

LIONEL FENN

ACE BOOKS, NEW YORK

This book is an Ace original edition,
and has never been previously published.

BY THE TIME I GET TO NASHVILLE

An Ace Book/published by arrangement with
the author

PRINTING HISTORY
Ace edition/March 1994

ISBN: 0-441-00020-7

ACE®
Ace Books are published by The Berkley Publishing Group,
200 Madison Avenue, New York, NY 10016.
ACE and the "A" design
are trademarks belonging to Charter Communications, Inc.

PRINTED IN THE UNITED STATES OF AMERICA

10 9 8 7 6 5 4 3 2 1

! REALLY IMPORTANT WARNING
FROM THE AUTHOR !

Because this is the second part of a trilogy that has, in all, three books, there are certain parts of the First Part of this particular book that make reference to certain things that happened in all the Parts of the first book, ONCE UPON A TIME IN THE EAST.

Therefore, if you don't want to know what happened in that first book, you can do one of two things:

You can buy the first book and read it first before you read this book;

Or you can be really really careful what you read in the First Part of this book so you won't spoil the nuances of the first book when you get around to reading it;

Or you can forget the whole thing, throw caution to the wind, and just read this book anyway.

Okay, it was three things.

Sue me.

Thank you.

—Lionel Fenn

BY THE TIME I GET TO NASHVILLE

PART I

On the Road Again,

Without a Decent Map

CHAPTER 1

In the midst of a parched summer worse than any in memory, the streets of Amarillo were deserted and silent, not a single shadow cast by the buildings that lined them. Not a dog barked, not a child played, not a face was to be seen in any of the shop windows. Houses squatted like beaten men under burning whips, troughs were empty, fences peeled, and grass turned brittle. The infernal heat, ten days and nights without respite or promise, without a cloud in the white-hot sky, had finally driven everyone indoors, had sapped life and color from signs and gardens, had baked wood and brick and crumbling adobe until they were fierce to the touch.

Only a dust devil danced in the alley by the stable.

Oddly enough, there was no wind.

An hour passed at a dead man's crawl as the sun rose toward noon; another hour gone, and a wisp of a cloud drifted over, and was gone; a third hour passed before a black ghost, a crow, flew over town, wheeled once, and flew off.

An unnatural silence.

The air shimmered.

Shadows faded.

Then a man of slightly more than average height stepped slowly from beneath the overhang of the mercantile, his spurs calling softly as he stepped down to the ground, his footsteps muffled. He was dressed in black, and wore a low-crown black hat with a silver medallion band. His long coat didn't hide the silver-studded gunbelt, nor the holsters carefully and expertly strapped to his legs. His shirt was white and ruffled, his waistcoat silver-threaded, and the handles of his revolvers made of etched ivory.

His face was lean, touched by the seasons he had spent in snow and sun, and his hair flowed gracefully down to his wide shoulders. He might have been called plain, might even have been called ordinary. Except for his eyes, the black of a cave that had never seen a light.

He glanced up and down the boardwalk and his shoulders rose with a slow inhalation, a gathering of forces, a sign he was about as ready as he ever would be. A touch of a calm hand to his hat brim, a slip of his palm down a lapel, and he moved to the middle of the street without seeming to hurry.

Steady hands pushed his coat back and away from his guns.

He faced the glaring sun, smiling mirthlessly to himself at the flaunting of conventional wisdom. The smile was the only thing visible on his face, however, for his eyes were hidden deep in shadow.

He took a deep breath and flexed his fingers slowly.

The dust devil died.

A mongrel bounded out of an open doorway and charged playfully into the open, saw the man, and raced away, his tail tucked submissively between his scrawny legs.

The man in black watched the creature run, but he listened for the betrayal of the outlaw's gun.

He listened.

He waited.

And finally, with a quiet sigh of relief and resignation, he heard it:

The solid *click* of a revolver's strong hammer being drawn back by a thumb.

The man in black whirled, drew, and fired.

Click

The man in black whirled, drew, and fired.

Click

The man in black whirled, drew, and fired.

Clickety-click

The man in black started to whirl and draw, stopped half-way around, and scowled.

Clickety-click? he thought; what the hell kind of a gun goes clickety-click?

Too late, he remembered.

Too late, he recognized the curious double-*click* that belonged only to the sawed-off shotgun used only by the outlaw they called Hoppo Crankshaw.

He spun back, squinting into the sun, and saw the outlaw grinning back at him, not six feet away, the infamous weapon aimed squarely at his chest.

The man in black said, "This can't be, damnit, you're dead."

"Tell me about it," Crankshaw said.

And pulled both triggers.

CHAPTER 2

The man they call . . . Diego sat abruptly up with a silent shout when the shotgun's fiery blast engulfed his chest, froze when he realized it had been nothing more than a dream, then twisted the shout to a rather vocal, and loud, torturous groan when a similar explosion blossomed briefly in his right side. He fell back immediately, but another, also similar, explosion of fire in his head snapped him straight back up to a sitting position where the fire in his side forced swiftly back down into a lying position. His head, realizing it had been outgunned and was growing seriously dizzy and disoriented, settled for some subdued but insistent complaining as he closed his eyes, waited patiently for calm to sift through his system and his breathing to return to as close to normal as he could get it, and tried to figure out what, exactly, was real, and what, exactly, still lingered of the nightmare he had had.

The pain, unquestionably, was authentic. Though the fire in both locations had subsided to a grumbling throb, there was no doubt at all it wasn't just an echo of the dream.

The sonofabitch *hurt*.

He couldn't remember ever feeling quite so bad.

A few seconds of enforced concentration finally enabled him to recall that some time ago he had been winged across the right side of his head, an understated scratch that had turned out to be more trouble than it was worth, if only because the gauze patch usually taped there kept knocking his hat off.

The wound in his side was a little more serious, being as how it had put a hole in his body, but since he hadn't yet bled to death, he reckoned he had somehow been patched up and placed onto a bed that was, when he felt gingerly around him, not much wider than he was.

So far, so good.

A second or two more gave him the name of the man who had, on both occasions, shot him—Runny Waters, youngest and meanest member of the notorious Hoppo Gang operating out of the New Mexico Territory in the latter part of the nineteenth century. The fact that Diego had, in turn, plugged the young outlaw into not so blissful eternity after that second shot gave him small satisfaction; his side still burned like hell.

Nothing else occurred to him.

It was as if his brain had been numbed in several places.

What he needed to do, he decided, was see if he could sit up again, this time without bringing a bucket of tears to his eyes. That way, he'd know better where he was, who had taken care of him, and why he was wherever he was in the first place.

Easier thought than done.

Each movement, whether it was connected to his side or not, made his injuries protest, broke sweat across his brow, and gave birth to an annoying tic near the center of his abdomen.

Helplessness, in his particular profession, was something not only to be avoided, it was to be tarred, feathered, and run out of town on a rail, preferably with the train still running just a few feet behind.

He hated it.

He might even go so far as to admit that it unsettled him.

All right, he told himself, all right. There's nothing to be nervous about. You're obviously safe or you'd be dead by now. All you have to do is remember just why it is that you are safe and not dead.

He opened one eye.

An angel grinned back at him.

He closed the eye and thought, okay, so you're dead, it isn't the end of the world, you've still got a lot of years ahead of you, just a few more than you'd counted on, that's all. Gird your loins, strap on your guns, and make the best of it. After all, how bad can it be?

The angel touched his shoulder.

He stiffened.

He remembered something else.

He relaxed.

He opened the eye again and said, "Molly."

He glanced past the anxious face to the ceiling, slightly curved, patterned, and remarkably like those he had seen on private parlor cars attached to trains making their way from the Mississippi to wherever it was the trains were going. His gaze, augmented by the completely unintentional opening of the other eye, took in the wall nearest the bed, and noted that it was of solid wood paneling. He turned his head to the right and saw an identical bed on the other side of a narrow aisle, saw two elegantly delicate Chinese screens at each footboard, demurely cutting this area of the car off from the sitting section.

There were, when he stared, also what appeared to be quite a lot of bullet holes in the furniture he could see.

That's when he remembered it all.

That's when he closed his eyes tightly and said, a little hoarsely, "If we didn't get away, touch my leg. If we got away, touch anything else as long as it isn't my side."

The angel caressed his brow with a soft cool cloth, about as heavenly a sensation as anything he had ever felt outside the delicate ministrations of a young lady of his acquaintance who worked part-time at the Gold Swan Saloon in Phoenix, which was, he recalled further, just about the only thing heavenly about Phoenix. The rest of the time it was just hotter'n Hell.

As the cloth moved tenderly to his cheeks and neck, he allowed himself one final, albeit perhaps lengthy, reminiscence, if only because it allowed him to catch up on where he was, why he was here, and why he wanted so badly to return to where he had been when he had first seen the angel, even if the angel, at the time, hadn't been all that angelic.

Diego had traveled through Time.

More accurately, he had, in escaping an assault by the aforementioned Hoppo Gang in Santa Fe, taken hasty refuge in what he had thought at the time, around 1880, had been nothing more than an odd-looking train. He quickly discovered, however, that the train wasn't really a train as he knew trains to be. That is, it looked almost exactly like a steam locomotive on the outside, but inside it had actually been transformed into a fully operational Mobile Chronometer Vehicle whose official technical name was the Time Thing.

He had been skeptical, then surprised, then astounded, then really annoyed.

Especially when the Time Thing had taken him away from Santa Fe.

In more ways than one.

Subsequently, at the point of one of his Diego Specials, he learned that the Time Thing had been created but not perfected by Virgil Lecotta, and Driven by his able assistant, Molly Thane. They had ended up in New York City sometime during the latter years of the twentieth century, of which Diego had not been then and was not now terribly impressed. It made no difference that it was Virgil's and Molly's Time; he still wasn't impressed.

People shot at him in his own Time; people shot at him in New York. And New Jersey, for god's sake.

It was not his idea of an historic occasion, that occasion being the traveling through Time; his idea of an historic occasion was getting paid without having to shoot the guy that was supposed to have paid him.

The last thing he remembered, aside from the Time Thing thing, was finally having it out with Runny Waters, who had hitched a ride to the future and had ensnared the volatile emotions of Virgil's ambitious but a little dense sister, Angel. After the shoot-out, and the resultant wound caused by a bullet passing through his body, Molly and Virgil had gotten him back into the TT and . . .

Home, Diego thought, his heart racing a little; the plan was, they were going to take me home.

He shifted on the bed, reopened his eyes and smiled when Molly pulled away, startled. Smiling wasn't something he did very often. You smile too much, the bad guys don't think you mean it when you point a gun at them.

"We got away," he croaked dryly, and coughed himself into a spasm that reignited the fire.

Hastily Molly put aside the damp washcloth and held a glass of water to his lips. Not precisely his liquid of choice in such circumstances, or any other save being in the middle of a vast desert, but she couldn't have known that, and it was, all in all, cool, wet, and soothing. He just hoped it wouldn't become a habit.

"We got away," he repeated when she took the empty glass back.

"We did," she answered proudly.

She was a lovely young woman, not that much shorter than he, with short fair hair, dark blue eyes, and a face just rounded enough to make a man's fingers itch. She wore, as she had at their first meeting, a snug-fitting union suit green enough to shame a spring lawn, with dizzying gold curlicues and designs across her chest and shoulders. He had finally figured out it was some kind of official Time Traveling uniform since Virgil wore the same stupid outfit. Including a ridiculous pair of gold-and-green boots with toes flat enough to hammer nails with.

She was also the Driver of the TT.

Immediately, a question rose, clung to his tongue, and waited patiently while he lifted the sheet covering him and looked warily under. He was naked. Except for the large fresh padding taped across his wound, he was stark, staring, raving naked. He blinked, looked askance at Molly, who grinned boldly back, and looked back at the place where there hadn't been a hole until Waters had shot him.

"You lost a lot of blood."

"I expect so."

"But it wasn't as bad as it looked. I cleaned it, stitched it up a little, and in a few days you ought to be able to move around fairly easily." She grinned again. "I had medical training, in case you're interested."

He nodded, eased himself upward until, with her assistance, he sat somewhat awkwardly against the headboard, pillows fluffed and propped behind him, the sheet demurely cast across his waist. It took a while for an abrupt bout of nausea to subside, but eventually he was able to see and think clearly again. It was bad, this incapacitation, but certainly not as bad as the time he'd been ambushed and dumped off a cliff by a scruffy scoundrel he had been hired to run out of Dodge a few years back. That had broken a couple of bones on the way down, a couple more when he had landed in a shallow creek, and had damn near ruined his new suit. Luckily the broken bones were mostly ribs, so it had taken him only another month to track the bastard down and show him how it felt to fly off a cliff. Without a shallow creek at the bottom.

Justice had been done, he had collected his money from the marshal who hired him, and the marshal's second cousin on his wife's side had been extremely grateful, since the bastard had been her husband.

"Where's Virgil?"

Molly nodded toward the door—it looked like maybe silver, with a helmsman's wheel in the center—that connected the parlor car with the engine room. "Working."

Diego's smile was brief. "But we *did* get away."

"Of course. I just said so."

He looked between the Chinese screens, and saw that the red velvet, tasseled shades had been pulled down over the windows. He shuddered. The last time he had looked out there, there'd been nothing but a disgusting yellowish, greenish, tending toward purplish swirling fog. It had been even worse when they arrived in New York.

"Are you hungry?"

He shook his head. Carefully.

She nodded. "Okay."

Diego waited patiently for her to tell him more. For as surely as he was buck naked under the flimsy sheet, there was something more to tell. There had to be. There had been a problem with the TT, Virgil had fixed it, and supposedly they were now on their way back in Time to Santa Fe. But if Virgil was still in the cab, working, then maybe he hadn't fixed everything there was to fix, and Molly didn't have the nerve to tell him because it would upset him, so she tried to appear extraordinarily casual as she wrung the damp cloth out over a small silver-looking bowl.

When she finished, she made to stand.

Diego took her wrist.

She looked at him nervously.

He looked at her, questioning with a slight lift of an eyebrow.

The movement of her full lips might well have been a reassuring smile in some obscure society of which he was not aware; here, on the other hand, it looked as if she had just split a seam in her amazingly awful green underwear uniform.

"I used to know an actress," he said.

"Oh?"

"Yep."

"So?"

"She was a darn sight better than you."

"Oh."

Then, in a rush that stopped his breath in his lungs, he remembered something else.

He didn't want to remember it. Remembering things such as the thing he had just remembered tended, more often than not, to reinforce the idea that he was, despite all evidence and hope and a couple of prayers to the contrary, still in trouble.

What he remembered was the last thing he had heard before he had passed out, probably on this very bed.

It had been Virgil.

And Virgil had said, "Oops."

Slowly and with some trepidation, he placed his free hand against the wall beside him. Although he had not been in the TT very long the first time around, he knew that there should have been, and there certainly wasn't now, a faint but discernible vibration. The wall was still. Which meant, to his limited understanding of how this train traveling through Time business worked, that the TT wasn't moving. Either through Time, or on tracks.

His heart raced again, and he struggled to keep his lungs from matching it.

"Diego?" Molly said anxiously. "Are you okay?"

"We're there, aren't we?" he said, wanting to laugh in spite of the agony it would cause.

"If you mean we've stopped . . . yes."

He stared at her sideways. "We're not still in . . . New York, are we?"

"Oh no, heavens no."

Heavens no? He wished he could find his guns. Molly Thane, in the short time he had known her, had never said "heavens no." He doubted she even thought it.

"But we're still not in your Time, are we?"

"Hell no."

That was more like it.

He shifted again, held his breath in anticipation of pain, felt none, and sat straighter. The wound was obviously not as bad as he had feared. Except for all the hurting. It was, in light of the woman's reluctance to embellish her responses, about the only comfort he could find.

He cleared his throat. "Then we must be home."

She waggled her hand side to side.

"All right," he said amiably. He knew that the TT had its problems, none of which, thus far, had been insurmountable. Virgil was an amazing scientist of the self-taught variety. "You didn't make it all the way to Santa Fe, I don't mind. So where are we? Albuquerque?"

She shook her head.

"Denver?"

"No."

"San Diego?"

"Sorry."

"Thank god." He frowned. "Wichita."

Another shake of her head.

"Abilene."

"Nope."

"Cheyenne."

"Look, Diego—"

"No, don't tell me. Guessing keeps my mind off the pain." He rubbed his chin thoughtfully. "St. Louis? Dallas? Tucson? San Francisco? Lincoln? Kansas City?"

"Diego, please."

A little desperately, he jerked a thumb at the wall. "Are we still in America?"

She slipped her wrist from his grasp and pushed herself to her feet, dropped the bowl and cloth onto the other bed, and clasped her hands in front of her.

"You've traveled a lot, right?"

He nodded warily.

"You ever been to Nashville?"

"Nashville what?" He blinked as realization dawned, much like being clobbered with wet dough. "Jesus, you mean Nashville, Tennessee?"

Her answer was a shrug that gave him entirely too much information.

His mouth opened, closed, worked a little in indecision, and finally remained as it was. It was true that he had never been to Nashville, and only once in his life had he ever been that far east—during a turbulent time he seldom thought about and had no desire to remember—but he supposed it wasn't all that bad. Once he was more mobile, he could take a train—a *real* damn train—over to Memphis and make his way down the Mississippi to New Orleans. In fact, that would probably be the best thing all around. He liked New Orleans. It was while he had been in that wondrous city that he had received the message to go to Santa Fe to take care of the Hoppo Gang, and he wouldn't mind returning to the Mississippi port so he could clear up a few loose ends of business. Like shooting the guy who had sent him the message.

"I know what you're thinking," she said, sidling toward the engine room door.

"Do you?"

She nodded, turned the wheel, and opened the door. "It won't work."

"Why not?"

"Virgil!" she called tremulously. "Would you mind coming in here a minute?"

There was no response.

The smile aimed at him was strained.

"Look," he said flatly, "there is no problem that I can see if we're in Nashville. I can find my way around. It isn't as if we ended up on the moon."

"Virgil, damnit!"

"Money might be a problem, but a couple of card games should take care of that."

She left the room.

She came back. Alone.

"He's a little busy right now."

"Molly, get my clothes."

"I had to clean them. They were—"

He had no choice, much as he didn't like it—he gave her the look that had made him reasonably famous in his Time, which, he was beginning to fear, still wasn't this Time, considering all the time she was wasting not telling him the Time.

She paled.

"Tell me," he said quietly.

She swallowed. "It isn't exactly Nashville that's the problem, you see."

"I just told you it wasn't."

Her hands began scrubbing each other nervously until she glared and made them stop. "Look, Diego, it's kind of . . . sort of . . . well, it has less to do with the *where* part of the trip than it has to do with the *when* part of the trip."

He almost understood that, and that almost made him as upset as she was. "But you told me we weren't in the twentieth century anymore."

"We're not."

Oh lord, he thought.

"So we went back in Time to . . . when?"

Her hands pushed back through her hair; her hands fluttered around her waist; her hands clasped and unclasped and made a beeline back for her hair.

"Diego?"

He only looked.

"Back isn't exactly the way I would describe the direction we took."

"How. Exactly. Would you describe it."

Her right hand gestured vaguely toward the sitting area. "Well . . . forward?"

CHAPTER 3

"Let me get this straight."

"I'll do the best I can."

"What you're trying to tell me—"

"You're not going to shoot me, are you? I mean, I don't think Virgil would really appreciate—"

"Don't be foolish, Molly. You saved my life."

"Just so I know."

"Good. So, what you're—"

"What about Virgil?"

"What about him?"

"Are you going to shoot him?"

"Jesus, Molly, he saved my life too."

"Yeah, but are you going to shoot him?"

"I . . . no."

"Good. Thank you."

"Molly. Hush. Please. Thank you. You see, what I'm trying to figure out here, without losing my mind, is that what you're trying to tell me is that your present was my future while we were in New York."

"Right."

"But now we're in *your* future, which is farther along in *my* future. And to make things worse, which they can't possibly be, we're not in New York anymore. We're in Nashville."

"Right."

"So what you're saying is that *my* future is now *longer* than *your* future, both of which are, actually, the present. In terms of where we are now, which is in the future."

"Right."

"*Our* future, this time."

"Right."

"Do you have any idea how far into the future you managed to take us?"

"A little. It's kind of vague, but I could give you some round numbers."

"How round?"

"Two, three hundred years."

"That round?"

"Give or take."

"Do you remember when, a couple of hundred years or so ago—Jesus!—I asked you not to bother to try to explain the things we both knew I wouldn't understand because I was from your past, your present being my future?"

"Very clearly."

"Is there anything about this—let's call it an accident so I don't feel strongly about hurting anybody—that you could explain that I would understand?"

"I . . . I don't think so. Not really."

"Thank God."

"Virgil might, though. He's better at this than I am. I'm only the Driver, remember? I just steer the damn Thing based on his complicated calibrations, calculations, and the theoretical physical law programs he's got programmed into the Vehicle's computers. One of which, I might add, is the one you shot back in Santa Fe and got us into this mess in the first place."

"Get my clothes."

"Jesus, Diego, don't shoot him."

"Lady, I am naked under this sheet, and I'm not about to listen to a long explanation, most of which I won't understand anyway, from a baldheaded guy, without something on."

"Okay. Sure. I can dig it."

"And while you're at it, bring my guns."

CHAPTER 4

Virgil Lecotta was indeed bald. Very bald. About as bald as a man can get without having his eyebrows trimmed and hot waxed. He was also quite tall, almost a head taller than Diego, broader across the shoulders and chest, paunchier in the belly, and wearing the same stupid uniform of unknown material except that it was just as green as Molly's. He also wore the same flat-toed boots. They did nothing for the ensemble. Or the people who wore them, for that matter.

At the moment, dubious sartorial splendor aside, he fidgeted on one of the two couches at the front of the parlor car while Diego sat in a plush wingback chair opposite him. Molly tried to sit on the couch, on the other one to Diego's right, on the floor, at the dining table by the screen, on one of the beds except that she couldn't hear anything back there, and on a small, stunning, marble-topped walnut cabinet in which a scant supply of liquor was kept. When she failed in all her attempts to appear nonchalant, relaxed, and don't worry about a thing, cowboy, this is normal procedure around the Mobile Chronometer Vehicle, she went into the bathroom and locked the door.

Diego, for his part, was still rather astonished at the way the woman had managed to clean the blood from his clothes, get the wrinkles out, and still leave them with that fresh-from-the-desert-and-not-dead-yet smell he liked so much. His side throbbed, yet not nearly as badly as it had when first he had awakened from his nightmare. That alone was curious; what unsettled him more was the realization, when he checked himself before dressing, that the wound wasn't as nasty as it had been when the bullet had initially punctured the flesh, nipped around a little, and popped out the other side. In fact, although it wasn't healed completely, neither did it look as if it had happened only yesterday. Or a couple of hundred years ago, depending on how he looked at it.

He couldn't stop pushing gingerly around the edges of the bandage.

"Interesting," Virgil said, sitting back, crossing his legs, folding his hands casually in his lap.

Diego looked at him without a word.

Virgil pointed. "That gunshot wound, I mean. It seems there are certain unexplained beneficial side effects to traveling through Time I hadn't counted on when I was fooling around in my father's basement with my experiments. Probably because they never occurred to me."

"Good for me," Diego said dryly.

Virgil attempted a smile. He was no better at it than Molly.

Diego let his palm and fingers run down the sleeve of his black jacket, the ruffles of his ruffled shirt, the silver threads of his waistcoat. Everything felt the same. He also ran through another death-check, which he reckoned should keep his confidence level up until Virgil got around to stopping his stalling and explaining what in the gloriously overheated hell was going on.

Finally he couldn't stand the fidgeting any longer. "Molly said this is my fault because I shot your computer, whatever that is, and don't bother, I wouldn't understand anyway."

Virgil's laugh was at once strained and relieved. "Oh, god, no, Diego, no. It's not your fault, believe me. I fixed all that—the Multi-Directional Circumlocator and stuff. We can move great now. It's just that we can't exactly pinpoint our target landing area. Chronologically, that is. Spatially, we're pretty good most of the time."

"Meaning?"

"The timer's shot."

"I shot the timer?"

Virgil shook his head tolerantly. "No, no! I mean, the basic instrument which guides the TT through the Time Continuum Flux is a little off."

Diego discarded all the words he didn't know, all the so-called theories he didn't understand, and said, "What?"

"I can't steer the damn thing," Molly shouted from the bathroom.

Virgil shrugged.

Diego let his fingers trail along the supple black leather of his gunbelt draped across the arm of the chair. They lingered at the ivory handle of one of his guns, O so tempting but moving on nonetheless.

Then he took a slow breath, held it, and wondered what in hell had happened to the old-fashioned, tell time by the sun method of getting around. By the same token, hadn't these people ever heard of maps? Which, suddenly, gave him another question he didn't want to ask, but he asked it because he figured he wouldn't understand the answer anyway:

"If you have the spatial ... if you ..." He scratched through his hair, closed his eyes briefly, and grunted. "If the part about getting where you want to go is okay, why are we in Nashville instead of Santa Fe?"

"Big deal!" Molly called.

Diego stared at the back door, which was at the end of an alcove formed by a storage room on the left and the bathroom on the right. "Why is she in there if she can hear everything out here?"

"Security," Virgil whispered.

"You can't shoot me in here!" she called.

Diego couldn't resist: "If I can hear you through walls that thin, I can shoot you through walls that thin."

Silence.

He almost laughed.

"Look," Virgil said earnestly. "We're just as much at sea as you are now. Figuratively speaking. If we were at sea, we'd probably be drowned. But we're not. We're at land, if you can say that. But the point is, you didn't understand half of our Time back in New York when you got there. And we probably won't understand half of Nashville now that we're here." He grinned. "We're even."

"No, we're not, we're lost."

"No, don't be silly. And unlike the last time, I know exactly what I need to fix it. It's no big deal, no sweat, I can have us up and running in less than twenty minutes. All I need is the right part."

Diego said nothing.

The silence drifted back into the car.

A silence broken only by the muffled noise of twenty-second-century Nashville floating ominously around the

TT—a subtle roaring in which no particular sounds could be identified. Not that such identification would matter; he had soon enough discovered the causes of similar noises back in New York and still didn't know what the hell they were. But at least he had these two people to explain what they were if he didn't really understand all the explanations.

Most of them, now that he thought about it.

Hardly any, if he was going to be truthful with himself.

But that was different.

This time, it seemed no one would be able to explain anything to anyone.

Still, it was, he admitted while Virgil worked himself up to another, no doubt largely incomprehensible, lecture, tantalizing. He had already peeked around a couple of the shades and on one side had seen nothing but a large stone wall dripping gleaming dark water. On the other side was parked an actual freight car that looked as if it had been through several wars and a cranky cattle drive. And the sky he could glimpse didn't tell him anything because it was dull silver. Silver with a few strands of curling black and glittering gold running through it. If it wasn't the sky, and he prayed devoutly that it wasn't, it was the ugliest ceiling he had ever seen in his life.

"Hey," Virgil said. "All things considered, we have to look on the bright side, right? At least you don't have that outlaw trying to gun you down anymore. You're safe, you're healing faster than a human being has a right to heal considering the wound you got, and all I have to do is go out there, get the part, and we're home free."

Perhaps the young man was right.

Unless . . .

"How do you know you can get what you want out there?"

Virgil clapped his hands in delight. "Because this is the future, Diego! And I'm pretty positive things haven't changed all that much since New York. You'll have to take my word for it, but there are some things, especially in electronics, which are fairly basic. They get fancier, but they're still pretty basic."

Diego considered. "You're sure about that."

"Damn right."

"You're absolutely positive you can get this part you need."

"Shit, yeah."

"So why haven't you gotten it?"

"Well," Virgil said uncomfortably, "that's the tricky part."

Diego just managed not to sigh. "You didn't mention a tricky part."

Virgil's discomfort brought him to his feet and into a pacing mode Diego had seen too often before. When the tall bald hefty young man passed him a second time, Diego reached out, grabbed his arm, yanked until he crouched in front of him, and said, "Tricky as in, it's closely guarded by a hundred pissed-off Sioux warriors? As in, it's locked in a safe whose walls are two feet thick? As in—"

Molly flung open the bathroom door and stepped into the alcove. "As in, he hasn't got any money to pay for it, that's as in."

Virgil slumped onto the floor like a deflated green balloon, his back against the couch, his face etched with misery. "It never occurred to me."

Diego stared at him in disbelief, even though he knew he shouldn't be surprised, knowing Virgil as he did. "Needing money never occurred to you?"

Molly snorted, but sat beside Virgil anyway, a comforting hand upon his leg. "It's okay, Virge. We'll—"

"Virgil."

"—figure something out. It's not as if we're in a foreign country, is it?"

Diego disagreed, but held his tongue. It was, as a matter of personal and unpleasant experience, exactly as if they were in a foreign country. The language sounded right but didn't mean anything; the customs were almost but not quite familiar; and everyone out there would probably look at these three and wonder what sort of asylum they'd escaped from—a man wearing a fancy black suit and six-guns, and two others dressed in awful green underwear.

He leaned back, eyelids drooping, foot bobbing just hard enough for his spurs to *ching* softly.

This whole thing reminded him of the time he had been chased by a couple of half-drunk but determined hired guns into Blackfoot territory. He had had some previous dealings with the Comanche, Cheyenne, Sioux, and a couple of really foul-smelling Apache who tended toward kilts and crooked

top hats, but these Blackfeet were a different people altogether. Although he had managed to lose his pursuers without
much effort, the braves who had subsequently picked up his
trail and attempted to capture him for no other reason than his
very presence on their land offended them were able to run
him down in a couple of days. It had taken most of his available ammunition and a ton of arm-wearying hand signals to
convince the tenacious band he was innocent of whatever it
was they thought him guilty. Once that had been established,
they traded an armload of beaver pelts for his horse. He
hadn't planned on that; he'd been trying to give them his saddle blanket. And it had taken him two weeks, a mountain
lion, and some truly unpalatable local natural fodder to find
his way to the nearest white man's outpost, where a French-
Canadian trader cheated him on the price of the pelts.

What had been an otherwise humiliating and humbling
experience had been soothed only when, a year later, he returned and shot off the trader's left ear. For nothing. Personal
satisfaction, in his business, was sometimes worth more than
all the gold in California.

"The way I figure it," he said at last, since the others
clearly weren't going to say anything that made any sense, "is
that we'll have to figure out what we got in here that we can
use for trading, then—"

Someone knocked on the door.

By the time Virgil and Molly were on their feet, Diego had
uncrossed his legs and unholstered his right-hand gun. He
kept it on his thigh, and looked to Virgil.

"Company?"

"Impossible. No one knows we're here."

Molly slapped his arm. "We're sitting in a train, for god's
sake. How's anybody not going to notice a goddamn train?"

Another knock, a little louder, more insistent.

"But we're—"

The knocking became an impatient, and one might even
say petulant, pounding that didn't let up, and Diego, seeing
that the couple wasn't going to answer the summons anytime
within the next hour or so, pushed himself from his seat,
waited until the stiffness in his side subsided, and made his
way slowly to the door.

The upper half was glass, but so begrimed and filthy from

its travels through Time that he could only see a shadow on the other side.

He sniffed, he eased the gun behind his back, slipped his finger through the trigger guard, and opened the door.

A man stood on the platform outside, pale against the dark grey, grimy, dripping, stained wall on the other side of the railing.

"Who's in charge here?" he demanded angrily.

Diego stepped aside and pointed with the gun to Virgil.

The man wasn't impressed, either by Virgil's bulk and height, or his stupid green underwear. "You? Well, you got twenty-four hours to get outta town, Bubba baby, or I'm gonna have to kill you."

"Is that so?" Diego said.

The man looked at him for the first time.

The man blinked rapidly enough to air out the car.

And before Diego could ask him to explain himself, the man threw up his hands, shrieked, and ran away.

CHAPTER 5

Slowly Diego turned from the door, walked to his chair, sat, stood and walked into the bathroom, a claustrophobic and dingy white affair with no more than a toilet, a sink, and a fairly dusty wall mirror into which he stared intently, leaning forward, turning his head side to side, finally stepping back and scowling. Traveling through Time hadn't changed his looks any. His shoulder-length hair was a little messed up, maybe, and his shirt ruffles weren't as fluffy as they might have been, but it was certainly nothing to scream about.

He sighed.

Easterners were a curious lot. They put the damnedest priorities on the damnedest things, even this far into his future, which he wouldn't have lived long enough to see even if he

had lived. Which, of course, he hadn't; otherwise, he'd be a
hell of a lot older, and probably drooling on a back porch, to
boot. Of course, he didn't much care thinking about how he
was, sometime in the past, already dead.

Which, now that he thought about it, he wasn't, really.

If he was dead in the past, he was reasonably certain he'd
be dead in the future, too.

It was, when he considered it further, a fairly cheerful notion when examined more carefully, though not in the mirror;
he could barely see his face there, much less the past. But if
he stayed in the future long enough, maybe he would actually
catch up to himself since he couldn't be dead in the past or
he wouldn't be alive now. That would be a hell of a thing. He
could actually tell himself to stay the hell off goddamn trains
since they were, although marvelously relaxing forms of
transportation, more damn trouble than they were worth. Even
if he hadn't had to buy a ticket.

Of course, if he was dead, but was still somehow able to
make it into the future, he might even run across his own
grave, which would probably mean he hadn't lived to see the
future, which he happened to be in now, so maybe he couldn't
be dead at all—another cheerful thought—until he realized
that if he wasn't dead, he wasn't in his own past either, one
way or the other, which meant that dying in the past was either impossible or damn hard. So if he . . .

He put a hand to his forehead and rubbed away the stirrings
of a headache. He seldom had headaches; usually only when
someone nailed him from behind with a hunk of wood, or he
had had too much of the good stuff to drink at Mistress
Milly's Emerald Crown Emporium over in Casper. But all this
thinking about being dead and alive and the future and the
past was getting to him. He figured he'd better knock it off
before his hair fell out.

"Hey!" Molly demanded. "You going to be in there all
day?"

He opened the door.

She stood with hands on hips and an expression that would
have curdled milk, if they had had any milk, which he
doubted. "It's about time. I thought maybe you'd died in
there."

He checked the mirror. "I don't think so."

"Well, you took long enough."

"I was thinking."

"That's what they always say." She turned back toward the sitting room. "C'mon, cowboy, time's a-wasting. We have to get moving."

Diego felt a ghost of a chill walk his spine. "Wait a minute."

She looked over her shoulder.

"This isn't going to be like the last Time, is it? Where we only have twenty-four hours to get something fixed or we all turn to jelly?"

She laughed. "God, no. I just don't feel like sticking around here any longer than I have to. Being in the future is one thing; being in a future Nashville is something else."

His brow creased as he stepped into the alcove. "Why? What's the matter with Nashville? Always heard it was a nice place. A little dull, maybe, but nothing to keep your grandma from."

A glance at the door, then.

"On the other hand, that fella there, he didn't dress like he was from a dull city."

In fact, the stranger had been a pale-skinned youth of fairly average height, average musculature, with deep brown hair dripping from under a garish beaded headband in greasy tangles down past his shoulders. Aside, however, from a glittering leather loincloth pleasantly if somewhat amateurishly embroidered with the sign of the running stag, tan fringed boots of rough rawhide that reached to mid-thigh, and a long necklace of bulbous colored beads around his neck, he had been pretty much naked.

"Man, he didn't dress like he was from anywhere," she said, plopping onto the couch beside Virgil. She thumped his arm. "Forget him, okay? The important thing is, can we get out and do whatever?"

Virgil stared at her forlornly. "But what about the money?"

"We'll think of something," she said, patting his hand solicitously. "Won't you, Diego?"

With a grunt, he told them he had no doubt he would be able to help get the money needed to purchase the part to fix the timer. Cash, for him, had seldom been a problem. The problem seemed to be getting to the place where the money could be gotten to purchase the whatever the hell it was required to fix the timer: if everyone reacted to him the way the white Indian did, it would be like trying to get to the saloon through a panicked buffalo herd.

" 'Course, it may not have been me," he added.

Virgil scowled and snapped his fingers. "Well, I'm certainly not anything to scare a kid with, damnit. It can't be me."

"Maybe they've never seen a woman before," Molly answered sourly.

Virgil closed an eye and thought about it.

"God," she muttered.

"You know," Diego told them as he eased into his chair, "every time I went to a place I'd never been before, I always made it a point to do a couple of things. First, I introduced myself to the local sheriff, except when he was the problem. Second, I always took a walk around the place, just to see what I could see. It helped in case I had to get somewhere faster'n what I thought I had to. Third, I always had a drink and played a couple of hands in the local saloon. Never been in one where the bartender didn't tell me pretty much what I needed to know before I attended to business."

He finished with a sharp nod.

Molly curdled the milk again. "Your business," she said tightly, "was killing people."

"Never killed an innocent person," he answered without heat.

"You—" She turned away, turned back, turned away, turned back and grabbed Virgil's arm before she fell off the couch. "Do you remember me telling you about that college course I took?"

He did. It wasn't a pleasant memory. The course dealt with American mythology, of which he was evidently a part, and the idea that he was a myth was somehow less disconcerting than annoying; it implied that he hadn't existed the way he did exist, which would have been news to people like Hoppo Crankshaw, who didn't exist anymore, but not because they were myths. He also remembered that her course, and the book Virgil had read about him when the hefty tall bald young man was much younger and had a lot more hair, didn't say what had finally happened to him. In a way, he was glad he didn't know how he was to die; in another way, it might have helped him plan for the future. Which, he reminded himself glumly, was about all he had these days, since all these days were in the future and entirely without his say-so.

"What's the point?" Virgil asked.

"The point is," she said to Diego, "how do we know you won't pop someone out there? We knew the rules back in New York. We don't know the rules here."

"That," he answered, still without heat, "is what sheriffs and saloons are for." He leaned forward. "Molly, it ain't my business that's bothering you. You've already seen me. You already know me. You know I don't 'pop' people without reason, and pay. You also know the rules were different back then, back in my Time." He paused. "So. You want to tell me?"

"What's going on?" Virgil asked.

Molly lowered her gaze to the floor and shook her head glumly. "I think ... I don't know. It was exciting when we got here, you know what I mean? The future and everything? But I've been wondering about ... I don't know. I think I'm feeling now the way you did, back then. In New York."

Diego nodded thoughtfully.

"How do you feel now?" Virgil asked.

"Now that it's over," Diego told her, "I figure it wasn't so bad. I had a little help, if you remember."

"Yes, but we're all new here."

He pointed to the window over her shoulder. "But I go someplace new all the time. It's part of my ... what I do. I expect you never did much of that, though, did you?"

When she looked up, she was smiling. "No. Not really."

"Hey," Virgil complained. "I'm lost."

"Exactly," Diego said.

Virgil's lips quivered.

Molly's smile became a grin.

"So now," Diego said, pushing decisively to his feet, "it's my turn." He plucked his hat from the chair-side table. "Virgil, you show me what it is we're looking for. Then I'll show you how we'll get it. Like the lady said—time's a-wasting."

Virgil, confusion still crawling over his features, led the way into the operational hub of the Time Thing—a long room which would have been the fuel hopper if there had been any coal or wood to fuel the engine. The walls were covered with metal things and lights and screens and dials and switches and gizmos Diego hadn't understood when he had first seen them, didn't understand now, and probably would never understand, which was all right with him since, when he got back home, he'd never need the information anyway, what with electricity and computers being at the stage they were in Santa Fe at the time, which was new and nonexistent. Well, maybe a couple of Indians he knew might get it, but only after they chewed on a peyote button, smoked some loco weed, and scalped a couple of jackrabbits.

Virgil leaned over a narrow shelf midway up the right-hand wall, pulled open a small perforated metal hatch, and reached inside. "You see," he explained, "all computers have what we call chips inside. It's how they get, store, process, and lose the information you tell them to hang on to." He looked at Diego. "You follow?"

"Nope."

Virgil shrugged. He was used to it. He pulled out his hand and opened it. Nestled in his palm was a tiny square black thing with tiny pointy metal legs. It appeared to Diego that a few of the legs were missing, just about where part of the tiny square black thing was missing.

He nodded. "When I shot—"

Virgil dropped the tiny black leggy thing onto the shelf. "That's right. When you shot the ... how shall I put it so you'll understand? ... the main gizmo, which I call the Sheriff because it monitors the rest of the equipment ... you nicked the clock, too. That"—he pointed to the black square—"is called a chip. For the Mobile Chronometer Vehicle, it acts as a timer. It tells us when we are and when we're going. Or it used to, anyway."

"Don't you have any extras?"

Virgil pointed at the hole in the console that Diego's bullet had made. "Blew 'em all to hell, pardner, when you shot the Deputy too. When I fixed the other stuff, I never saw the nick in the clock. Since it seemed to be working, I never thought to check it."

Diego poked at the chip with a finger. There was no way in hell such a tiny black leggy thing could hold all the stuff

Virgil said it held, but he wasn't going to argue the point. He knew what he knew, and the kid knew what the kid knew, and when you put it all together, he figured what it added up to was a number he had no idea what it meant.

The headache stirred.

He rubbed his forehead.

"You said you figure you can get one of these things out there?"

Virgil nodded eagerly. "A city this size, it can't be more than a block or two away."

"They sell these things in stores?"

"Sure."

"Why?"

Virgil pulled open a drawer in the shelf and swept the chip into it. "For your computer."

"I don't have one. I don't even know what it is."

"Well, in the past—my past, not your past—just about everybody had one. You know, they did your checkbooks, kept your bank balance, stored your recipes, things like that."

Diego turned his hat over in his hand. "Ran out of pencils, huh?"

Virgil said nothing.

"It was a joke," Diego said.

Virgil just looked at him.

Diego decided this was no time to explain jokes to a man who held his future, his past, and his present in his meaty paws. Virgil was a nice guy, good to have at your back in a pinch, but there were times when he wanted to smack him upside the head, just to find out if he could hear any echoes.

"Yo!" Molly called from the front.

"Yo?" Diego said.

"It's an expression," Virgil explained, heading for the door.

"What's it mean?"

"Depends on how you say it."

Yo, Diego thought; yo. He had a feeling that if he said it, he'd sound like an idiot.

Instead: "Virgil, what do you figure it's like out there?"

"I guess we'll see soon enough." The bald young hefty tall man closed and sealed the hatch-door behind them.

Someone knocked on the door.

Molly jumped up from the couch, grabbed an ashtray from

the table, and tucked the weapon behind her as she hurried into the alcove. Diego wanted to caution her, but before he could say a word, she had the door open.

The white Indian was back.

He had brought a friend.

"See?" The white Indian pointed at Molly. "What did I tell you?"

The friend was a dark-haired woman, about as young as her companion, but wearing a pair of white fringed boots, a short fringed skirt of vivid blue, a matching blouse with enough rhinestones on it to blind a rock, and a stiff-looking western hat equally decorated, only there the rhinestones were of several different colors. All of them were awful.

"It's a woman in green underwear," the girl said, rubbing a finger under her pug but attractive nose. "So what?"

Molly shifted just enough to send Virgil rushing down the aisle to clamp his hand onto her elbow.

"But they're not supposed to be here!" the white Indian declared indignantly. "Somebody finds them, I don't get my Bless this week."

The girl shut him up with a disgusted look and stared at Virgil. "You always wear green underwear?" She giggled. "Love the feet, though."

"What do you want?" Virgil demanded, looming over Molly's head.

The white Indian scowled. "Hey, straight, I already told you, huh? You got twenty-four hours to get outta town, or else."

Virgil wasn't impressed. "Or else what?"

The girl pushed her hat back and planted her hands on her hips, which just happened to be wearing a two-gun holster which, instead of the two revolvers usually found in such accessories, held two gleaming machetes with curved teak handles tipped with glittering yellow tassels. "Or else you're sliced, Bubba baby." She winked. "I don't lose, you know."

Molly, struggling to free her arm at the end of which was the hand that held the ashtray, looked her over and said, "Blow it out your ear, sister."

The white Indian paled.

The cowgirl stepped back, lowered her hands, and flexed her fingers. "Lady lady," she said, deepening her voice and

shaking her head, "you just ran outta time in my town." She
squinted. "Draw."

Molly held out her free hand. "Draw what?"

The cowgirl smirked. "Guess you're plumb outta luck, ain't
you, lady lady?" She took a slow, deep breath and wiggled
her fingers over her machetes. "On the count of three, you're
gonna die, visit the screen, blow the tube. Your ass is grass,
and I'm the digital trimming blade."

The white Indian giggled.

Molly, realizing the cowgirl was serious, tried to step back,
but Virgil was in the way. "Do you mind?" she said over her
shoulder.

"One," said the cowgirl.

"C'mon, Moll, get a grip. You really think she's going to
do anything?"

"Two."

The white Indian drew a yellowhead tomahawk from his
belt and spit on the obviously sharpened edge. His grin was
less human than it was wolfish, and hungry.

"Virgil."

"Three," said Diego, stepping up so the pair on the platform could see him.

And his gun.

With the hammer cocked.

A dramatically tense moment passed.

Then the white Indian yelped.

The cowgirl shrieked.

The two of them bounded off the platform, their screams
mingling into a spritely musical echo of unbounded except for
the walls terror.

Diego immediately shifted the gun to his left hand, pushed
his way outside, grabbed one of the climbing rungs that led to
the roof, and swung out so he could see down the train. The
pair had just rounded the front of the engine, neither of them
looking back.

"Virge? What did she mean by 'my town'?"

"I don't know, Moll."

Neither did Diego. But when the screams finally faded, he
had an unpleasant feeling it wouldn't be long before he found
out. Not that he wanted to. Sometimes Life just turned out
that way. You learned things you didn't want to learn, you

didn't learn things you should have learned, and the folks who tried to teach you didn't always have your best interests at heart. What puzzled him as he holstered his revolver was another feeling—a curious one that suggested for no reason he could pin down that those two weren't really serious about wanting to kill him and his friends. They were playing. Pretending. Acting. Depending on intimidation and fear to do most of their work for them. Although, he thought further, how that half-naked white Indian could intimidate anyone was something he supposed only the future could explain.

"Diego?"

He glanced to his right.

"You going to hang out there like that all day, or what?"

He swung easily back to the platform. "Just checking, Molly."

She nodded sharply. "Good. So while you're checking, you want to tell me why everyone around here screams whenever they see you?"

CHAPTER 6

They double-checked to make sure the Center of Operations Room hatch was sealed, the liquor cabinet was locked, and the bathroom was locked, from the outside. Then Molly told them to hang on a minute, and rustled around in the storeroom until she found what she believed were suitable defensive weapons, just in case they ran into more cowgirls and white Indians who, this time, didn't run away.

Virgil rolled his eyes. "Molly, a lamp isn't going to cut it."

"It will if I hit someone."

Reluctantly, however, she set the three-foot-base faux Tiffany lamp on the side table beside what had become known as Diego's chair, and asked, somewhat sourly, if the knife would be all right.

"It's a butter knife," Virgil answered sadly.

Molly ran the rounded blade lovingly over her thumb. "I could sharpen it."

"Sure. And while you're at it, stick a better handle on it because it's only two inches long, for god's sake. How the hell you going to get close enough to stab anybody with it, ask him to dance?" He rolled his eyes again. "Of course, maybe butter's gone sentient in a couple hundred years, you never know."

Molly threw the knife on the couch. "Y'know, Virge—"

"Virgil."

"—sarcasm is not one of your strong points."

Diego, meanwhile and after a brief, futile prayer to the Deity to stop kidding around and let him wake up, had strapped on his gunbelt, checked the load in each revolver, made sure his spurs were still sharp enough to slice leather, and put on his hat.

The two stopped bickering.

They knew what the hat meant.

Diego knew what the hat meant too, which was mainly to keep his long hair from flying into his eyes in case someone shot at him, but he respected their own personal interpretation, nodded once, and stepped back onto the platform.

"I'm a little nervous," Virgil whispered to Molly as she retrieved the knife from the couch.

The TT had landed, if that was the word for whatever the TT did when it stopped traveling through Time and ended up wherever it was going to end up, with its parlor car platform not a foot away from a stained greystone wall. Diego touched it with a finger, and grimaced—not only was the wall warm, it dripped with a mottled black grime that felt oily and gritty. He wiped his finger on the railing and stepped down to the right, to a gravel path that led between the TT and the freight car he had noticed earlier. There was no railroad or company designation on the side, and when he looked forward, he saw at least a half dozen others, including a tanker and a coal car, settled on rusted crumbling tracks.

He dropped into a crouch—no one, as far as he could see, hid beneath the TT, and, in the other direction, all he could spot were the wheels of at least two or three more trains lined up on the other side of the freight. Puddles and pools of brackish water shimmered in the colorless light.

He rolled his shoulders and flexed his legs to keep himself alert and loose.

Without waiting to see if the others would follow, he straightened and headed toward the engine, a gleaming locomotive with vivid red and gold stripes along its sleek boiler. The engineer's cab appeared open, as it should have been, but he knew that was an illusion. Behind that illusion, in better times when the damn Thing worked, sat the most skilled Driver in Time Traveling history.

"Really nervous," Virgil whispered somewhere behind him.

With a sharp gesture, Diego signaled him to shut up. He suspected the cowgirl and the white Indian were long gone from this curious place, but he hadn't lived as long as he had doing what he did for a living without first making sure there was no one around to cut him off in his prime, which, he figured, ought to last until he was too old to do anything but pretty much drop dead of old age.

Other than the muted din coming from somewhere outside, there was no sound but the soft crunch of his boots on the gravel and the whispered *ching* of his spurs. The air was warm, but not uncomfortably so, and when he checked above him, he was pleased to see that the dull silver laced with black and gold was, in fact, the ugliest ceiling he had ever seen in his life and not the sky, as he had feared. A ceiling supported by massive, fluted, concrete pillars banded every ten feet in iron as much in disrepair as the tracks.

He eased himself around one, and stood at the front of the engine, scratching his neck lightly.

Directly ahead, the ceiling merged downward into a disgustingly filthy, pock-marked wall. In the wall was a double-height, double-wide metal-looking door with a pitted brass, waist-high bar across it, and no indication of how the other trains had gotten in here. The tracks ended when the cars did.

There seemed to be no question but that this part of the station, if station it was, had been walled off.

Virgil and Molly crunched up beside him.

"So what do you think?" she asked.

He thought he would rather be in Santa Fe, New Orleans, Denver, Cheyenne, St. Louis, Moon River, or even San

Diego; he thought he didn't much care for the noise that filtered through the slightly open door—it smacked of too many people crammed into too small a space with too many mechanical things vying for room with the people; he thought he would like a pretty stiff drink about now, a good round of poker, and a dancehall girl hanging on his arm, leering at him suggestively and throwing him off his game.

"Looks like the exit," is what he said instead.

Molly nodded and turned to Virgil. "See? He said he had to get the lay of the land first. Pretty good, isn't he?"

Diego also thought that Molly was much better at sarcasm than Virgil, a doubtful skill at best these days, considering he had the guns and she only had the butter knife.

"I still want to know what that bitch meant by 'my town,' " she added. "And why this place is off-limits." She looked around, crouched to peer under the freight train, noted the other cars, and said, "It could be a museum, what do you think?"

"You don't think they use trains anymore?" Virgil asked with a distinct melancholy.

"Two hundred years in the future," she reminded him. "Don't you think they've improved things by now?"

Diego, while he was willing to consider the possibility of a world without trains making their slow way across the landscape, knew this was no museum.

The condition of the cars, the tracks, the fact that the tracks didn't go anywhere except under the cars—

It wasn't a museum.

It was a graveyard.

And for some reason, that bothered him more than it probably should have.

But, for the time being, time being what it was for him lately, he was less concerned with that than he was the screaming and the shrieking and the running away. The outlaws he had chased in his own time tended to flee as well, except when they wanted to fight or kill or maim or dismember him, but they never screamed or shrieked. Not even close. They just got on a horse and rode off, once in a while tossing the odd stick of dynamite in his general direction.

And while he wasn't a particularly vain man, his recent check in the mirror had proved that Time Travel hadn't some-

how made him as ugly as that miner he'd once run across in
northern California, the one who kept claim jumpers at bay
simply by showing up now and then and letting them get a
good look at him. Diego shivered. It was a sight he hoped
never to see again in his life. The man was so bad, he made
outhouses look comfy.

"A plan," Virgil said then. "We should have a plan."

"Jesus, Virgil," Molly complained. "What's to plan? We go
out there, we look around for a place that sells chips, we get
the one we need, we come back, you put it in, you fire up the
TT, and I Drive us the hell out of here."

"Good plan," Virgil said.

"Thanks."

Diego started for the door.

"But how are we going to pay for it?"

"If we can't pay for it, we'll steal it."

Diego would have braced himself against the wall and
peered around the jamb if the wall hadn't been so disgusting
and drippy, and covered, now that he looked more closely,
with occasional patches of a kind of foul brown moss that
made his stomach tighten just to look at it.

Instead, he settled for a deep breath, a minor but psycho-
logically necessary adjustment of his gunbelt, a correction of
the fall of his jacket to hide the guns from public view, and
a settling of his hat more comfortably over his brow.

"He's doing the hat thing again," Molly said.

"Then I guess we'd better get going."

Diego took a step.

"Wait!"

Diego stopped.

Virgil hurried to stand next to him. "Do you have any idea
what's going on here?"

"Thought I did."

"No, no, not that," the bald tall hefty young man said excitedly. "I mean, do you realize we're actually going to step
out into the *future*? I mean, we're going to be the first ones
in the history of mankind to actually *be* where no one has
ever *been* before!" He shook himself. "My god, this is practically historic!"

"Well, Jesus," Molly said, "don't wet your pants or anything. We're not going to be here that long."

"That's not the point."

A sudden bright smile illuminated Molly's face, and her voice softened. "I know. It's great, isn't it?"

"Great isn't the word for it." Virgil looked to the ceiling. "How about 'momentous'?"

Molly nodded vigorously. "Stupendous!"

"Colossal!"

Molly threw her arms around him and beamed into his face. "Extraordinary!"

Virgil kissed her. "Unique!"

"Wet," said Diego.

Still in their spontaneous clinch, the pair stared at him.

Diego jerked a thumb upward. "Wet. The ceiling is dripping all over me, and I'm getting wet." He aimed the thumb at the door. "Mind if we head out?"

"God," Molly said, "maybe we should say something, y'know? Like Armstrong did when he landed on the moon."

"Good idea," Virgil said. "Something short but powerful, and easy to memorize so the press doesn't screw it up."

Diego said, "On the moon?"

They stared at him again.

Diego closed his eyes briefly. "Never mind. I don't want to know."

His companions unclinched and stood behind him eagerly, heads bobbing with excitement.

"You first," Molly told him.

"Absolutely," Virgil agreed. "You've come the farthest, you should be the first."

Diego didn't argue.

He pushed the door open a few inches more.

Molly failed to contain a squeal; Virgil laughed quickly.

Diego stepped out of the cavernous room.

Molly and Virgil crowded after him.

"Damn," Diego said quietly.

"Good . . . god," Virgil whispered hoarsely.

And Molly Thane was speechless.

CHAPTER 7

Diego, with years of sneaking-around training behind him, knew a deserted and no longer used staircase when he saw one. It was wide, of worn marble, and a good twenty levels high. The ceiling, as much as he could tell through a thin mist that clung and drifted there, was of vaulted and elaborately carved stone; and the walls were disturbingly similar to the wall he had just left on the other side of the door. Which is to say, they were pretty disgusting, and no way in hell was he going to touch them.

Having established that, he proceeded to climb upward, keeping in the center, keeping his gaze on the diffuse white light he could see at the top. Halfway up, he realized that some of the light came from small bulbs embedded in some clear but grungy material spaced every fifteen feet or so in the lowering ceiling.

Molly and Virgil, following Diego's expert example, trailed behind him, noting as they did the faded framed posters affixed to the walls on either side, framed posters which announced in garish and tawdry lettering barely worthy of the term concerts of every possible description save chamber music, all said concerts to be performed in the Palatial Ol' Opry Arena, free admission, bring your own chairs and clubs. There were no dates mentioned. In fact, there were no specific acts, musical groups, or touring string bands mentioned. There weren't even any pictures. Just words, and not all of them were spelled right.

Between the posters, and beneath the grime and moss Diego swore was watching him, was scrawled faded instances of sprayed graffiti, none of which were very legible, and none of which he figured would have made any sense anyway, especially the one that shakily proclaimed "Elvis Lives!", since the only Elvis he knew had been Elvis Lee Bob Billy Sessoms, a chunky Missouri bank robber of little repute who had been shot down by an irate barber in Laredo when he, Elvis, had attempted to rob the barber's shop since the bank had been closed, it being Sunday at the time. The only reason Diego knew about it was because he had arrived that very afternoon on business, saw the crowds, asked around, and rode right back out again. A community that shoots barbershop robbers on Sunday without benefit of a fair and just trial was not his kind of place. More so when they subsequently tied the body to the barber pole and made bets on how many times it would spin around before the dead guy's hat fell off.

Days were slow in Laredo.

Damn dull, too.

Just below the top of the staircase, he paused, listened for telltale signs of ambush and murder, then stepped all the way up and found himself in what had probably been the station's main waiting room. It was a modestly huge affair which had evidently seen many alterations in its time. To the left and right, doors hung on rusted hinges, shop windows had long since lost their glass, and he surprised himself by recognizing the gaping entrance to one of those elevator things. Tattered papers and ragged cloth were scattered across the floor; piles of dust, broken glass, and splintered wood made shadowy islands; and the ubiquitous and damned annoying water drips dripped from the ceiling.

And there, at the far end, a series of four double doors that, even at this distance, had clearly been boarded up on the outside.

From around the boards, and through the many cracks therein, panels of dull white light shone weakly into the station. Dust floated lazily through them. Once in a while one of them blanked out, as if something had passed by on the other side.

"It's like a tomb," Molly said quietly, shivering in the dampness.

"Boy, what stories it must have to tell," Virgil said reverently, turning in a slow circle as he looked upward, shading his eyes from the many drips that *ping*ed off the baldness of his pate.

Diego said nothing.

He strode cautiously onward, checking for movement at the doors, his ears attuned for the unusual and out of place even though he had no idea what in hell would be unusual and out of place in this place, and his hands close to his guns. This ancient, and no doubt once grand, railroad station did indeed feel like a tomb, and most likely had thousands of fascinating stories to tell, but his mind was focused on something more important just at the moment, something he didn't want to bring up just yet because the others were too engrossed in their reactions, too involved in their impending step into the real live future, too caught up in their conflicting emotions to even begin to wonder if those doors up there were locked.

When he reached the center pair, however, he realized that his concern had been for naught; if that cowgirl and the white Indian had gotten in, they had also gotten out. Which meant they had gotten out this way. Unless, of course, they were waiting in ambush in one of those deserted rooms and shops, or there was another exit of which he was unaware.

He shook his head.

He tested the right-hand door gingerly.

It moved.

He smiled without mirth.

"So what do you think?" Molly asked when they caught up with him.

"About what?" Virgil said.

"About those first words."

The young man, who was also tall and bald and reasonably hefty, shrugged. "I think Diego said it all back there."

Diego braced himself, and opened the door.

He said it again: "Damn."

PART II

Hang 'Em, Hi,

But Don't Waste the Rope

CHAPTER 1

While Diego had never been a dandy, and had never had an occasion to dress like one, he prided himself on maintaining a decent appearance when circumstances, like people not shooting at him, would permit. After all, when a man or woman or sheriff or governor of a territory hires you to do the job they expect you to when they give you money to do it, you don't show up looking like something they wouldn't even kiss in Texas. Nevertheless, despite the white Indian and the cowgirl, he had been afraid that, based on his sartorially harrowing experience in New York, his appearance, and that of his friends, might be too different for the Time. Which would ruin their plan of getting what they had to get so they could get out, because they'd attract too much attention.

Especially the green union suits, which Molly had explained were in her Time called, among other things, body suits, a term he usually reserved for that once-in-a-lifetime outfit you wore when you were one.

But when he stepped outside into the pleasantly warm air, he realized instantly that he didn't have a thing to worry about. At least not about his clothes.

He stood in a deep recessed entrance, a half dozen wide steps to the pavement fanning out ahead of him. As the others sidled out, he made a swift foray to the top of the steps, and checked the length and breadth of the extra wide street. Nodded curtly. Hurried back into the shadows and said, "Get me the hell out of here."

"Why?" Virgil asked.

"Look for yourself," he muttered, and jammed his hat

down over his eyes in what he already knew was probably a futile attempt to keep from going blind.

Directly opposite them was Nashville, in whatever century the Time Thing had managed to burp them into.

Although Molly said "Wow," and Virgil exclaimed "Oh boy," it was not, as far as Diego was concerned, a pretty sight.

The buildings were all extremely, impossibly tall, and of such an odd metal-and-glass-and-something else he couldn't name and didn't want to construction that he could have sworn that the one directly across the boulevard was supposed to resemble nothing less than a stylized, and pretty damn useless, guitar, and that one up there looked like a fiddle with a hell of a long neck, and if that one down there wasn't supposed to be a jew's harp clamped between a pair of blinding teeth, then he was in dire need of a new pair of eyes.

Which he suspected he needed anyway since every one of the buildings bristled with signs both large and small. The signs were primarily in neon. Bright neon. Flickering and buzzing neon. Practically shouting itself hoarse neon. The same bright flickering buzzing and practically shouting itself hoarse neon that all the other signs on all the shops, offices, and street corners they could see were made of. In colors that had never existed until neon had been invented. Colors that, as the signs were hung higher as the buildings grew taller, became blurred and illegible except when they weren't comprised of letters but amazingly lifelike pictorial representations of whatever it was they were representing, those pictures moving in such a realistic manner that Diego had to look twice to be sure the faces he saw up there, and over there, and on that damn thing floating down the street twenty feet above the ground weren't real.

When he was in New York, he had seen similar astonishments, but realized they had been only crude forebears of the miracles he witnessed now.

He still didn't like them, but he had to admit that the fellas who made them had certainly gotten better at it. As a matter of fact, the last time he had seen such intense light like this, he had told the bartender to cork the bottle, set up a tent outside town, and start working miracles, he was definitely in the wrong profession.

"Amazing," Molly said.

For just a moment, a brief snippet of time, he allowed himself to feel superior. He had been overwhelmed to the point of damn near passing out when he had seen what New York in the twentieth century looked like; he reckoned his friends were feeling the same way now.

"Well," Virgil said, somewhat breathlessly, "at least I won't feel like a jerk in my Time Travel uniform."

There weren't nearly as many people as Diego had seen in New York, but there were still enough to make him uneasy; and those who passed the station exhibited modes of dress as varied as the signs and buildings—rags that barely covered the scrawny bodies that held them, elegant evening clothes in hues of dark blues and darker greens that gleamed like velvet and satin, baggy suits and ill-hung dresses that appeared to be the universal fashion for those who toiled in the shops and offices.

But just as often an oddity drifted by—a man in a suit of pliable armor with braided peacock feathers in his helm; a redheaded woman wearing little more than a costume of silver ringlets that left nothing to any man's imagination if he had any, which Diego had, and it shocked him; a group of children wearing lifelike animal masks and spiked tails that protruded from holes in their pants; a quartet of men in monks' garb, right down to the sandals which, Molly pointed out, were trimmed in fur and what seemed to be sharpened toothpicks; a burly man and his female companion wearing plaid shirts, wide leather belts, jeans, and western boots and hats; an old woman with a paving stone strapped to her back.

Exhausted from all the observation, not to mention all the noise, Diego leaned a shoulder against the wall and shook his head. He didn't know what to say. This Nashville, this Tennessee, this once emerald isle of fabled civility and what Virgil had called down-home music had somehow taken a turn into an open mine shaft and landed on its head.

"My god!" Virgil exclaimed.

Startled, Molly grabbed his arm. "What?"

Diego only shifted his hat so he could see better, then shifted it back so he didn't have to see anything he didn't want to look at, which, considering what Virgil had seen, was just about everything.

There were automobiles here, too.

Or what may have been automobiles, it was difficult to tell since they resembled those ambulatory vehicles only in that they looked somewhat like them, but without most of the usual automobile characteristics, the most important of which was pretty much sticking to the ground.

For although the automobiles, in many sizes and many colors and some very bizarre shapes, moved determinedly along the street, they also floated above the surface instead of resting on their wheels.

"Wow," Molly said.

Not exactly the word Diego had in mind.

There appeared to be only two lanes—northbound, near the ground, and southbound, about twenty or thirty feet above those heading north. Every so often, a vehicle would swerve from one lane to another, twisting and darting like an exultant butterfly that had discovered the secret of a good sipping bourbon.

Diego snapped his fingers.

Virgil hurried over.

"How soon do you figure we can get what you need?"

Virgil's expression was that of an ordinarily healthy man who had just learned that he had only ten months to live, and all of it was going to be here. "I . . . I don't know. I thought it would be easy to find a store, you know? I didn't realize . . ." His left hand gestured helplessly at the garishly bleak scene before them.

"Doesn't help," Diego said dryly.

"Well, maybe . . ." Virgil took a step down and stared up the low hill toward its crest. "I suppose we could walk a little, see what kind of a district we're in. Maybe we can spot something that looks like what we want."

Diego nodded, shrugged one shoulder, nodded again. He had already noted that the sky was invisible. Not that Nashville needed a sky. All this light down here, it wouldn't make any difference if the sun was out or not because no one could see it anyway.

Rain, he figured, must be one hell of a surprise. Snow was undoubtedly out of the question.

Virgil scratched his bald pate thoughtfully. "Maybe we

could find a telephone booth somewhere and look it up in the yellow pages."

Diego looked at him.

The young bald tall hefty man raised his eyebrows in apology while, at the same time, saying that as long as *he* knew what it meant, Diego didn't have to. At least not this time.

Which was, all in all, fine with Diego.

"Why don't you ask somebody?" Molly said.

Both Virgil and Diego stared incredulously at her: "What?"

"Ask!" Molly repeated. "What's the matter, you think these people are Martians or something?"

"What's a Martian?" Diego whispered to Virgil.

"A monster or humanlike creature that lives on the planet Mars," Virgil whispered back.

"Yes," Diego answered.

"Jesus. Men."

Tucking her butter knife safely into her breast pocket, she stomped steadfastly down the steps, glared over her shoulder, and waited impatiently until they took the hint and joined her. Then she scanned the street in both directions, muttering to herself, before she finally pointed uphill, to the right. "That way," she declared.

"How do you know?" Virgil asked.

Her smile was brittle. "Intuition."

He nodded in the direction she wanted them to take. "So what does your intuition say about all that?"

That, being the signs. Not the ones in the windows of the guitars or the base fiddles or the snare drums, and not the ones on the whooshing-past vehicles, some of which had taken to whoosh past sideways, but the ones that protruded perpendicularly from the street-level shops—the lifelike animated ones that had women in elegant evening dresses taking showers in the backseats of old-fashioned convertibles, the ones that showed a rhinestone cowboy riding a bucking bronco whose legs were made of candy canes, the ones that declared in simple Nashvillian English the attraction of purchasing, at no extra cost to the consumer, a ticket to the world's greatest semi-indoor jungle this side of the Atlantic.

Or the one just at the top of the low hill that said *Computers! Old! New! You Want It, We Got It! And If We Ain't Got It, We Can Get It!*

With a huge winking arrow pointing toward a side street across the way.

"Oh," Virgil muttered.

She laughed kindly, took his arm, and marched him up the sidewalk, chattering softly and excitedly, and wondering if she should have brought her camera, no one was ever going to believe this.

Diego, who believed it all too well, narrowed his eyes, lowered his hat, and against his better judgment, joined them, half expecting the citizenry to break into hysterical screaming and shrieking and running away once he appeared in the light of day, or night, or neon, or whatever they called it around here.

But the pedestrians ignored him.

So did those who sat in small booths at the curb, hawking all manner of mercantile goods, none of which he recognized, although one looked remarkably like something he had seen on a Kansas cattle drive, the item in question being for the personal use of the cowboys who claimed to have standards about abusing cattle on their way to market. It looked disgusting then; it looked disgusting now. But then, so did the cowboys.

Nevertheless, they paid him no heed.

At least he thought they didn't.

Yet every so often he felt a gaze follow him, a glance ricochet off his shoulder, a sideways stare sneak around his hips. He told himself he was simply on edge, this being a new and strange and entirely outlandish place. Still, safety and a long life being always uppermost in his mind, he made sure Virgil stayed on his left and Molly on his right, figuring their green uniforms would get most of the attention, and he would be little more than an afterthought too late to catch up to.

Of course, the ruse probably wouldn't be as effective as the time he had donned the preacher's wife's mourning dress in order not to be damned to hell with a shotgun; but he reckoned it was better than the time he had donned the undertaker's suit when the preacher finally found out his wife didn't have a hell of an ugly visiting aunt. The preacher had seen right through that one after a while, probably because all the seams had split wide open. If it hadn't been for the undertaker's wife, and that empty coffin in the living room, he might not have gotten out of Waco alive.

Meanwhile, he did his best to understand just what it was he was looking at when he read posters plastered to places where there weren't any signs, and when he looked through the store windows he passed, which wasn't easy considering all the neon that kept blinding him, which, when he thought about it, was probably the idea anyway. But he doubted he would go into one of them just to find out what it was they were selling. Half the words he saw he didn't know, a quarter of them he couldn't figure out, and the rest of them simply made no sense at all as far as the English that he knew was concerned.

"Now what," Molly wanted to know, "is a Memphis Belle?"

She pointed to a blue-rimmed window in which, some-where in the midst of muted neon pulsating hearts and muted blossoming neon flowers, could be seen a moving, nearly three-dimensional image of a scantily clad woman whose eyes followed those who looked at her, and a few who didn't but really wanted to. Virgil suggested a futuristic lingerie shop. Diego, forgetting his not quite a vow not to step inside, stepped quickly inside, glanced around, stepped back outside, and said, "You ain't going to believe what they're selling in there. Right out in the open."

"Women," Molly answered.

Diego stared at her.

"I'm not a nun, you know. I've been around."

A pair of scruffy, barely dressed men bumped into them then, mumbling about getting shine, getting spheric, getting these damn funny dressed tours out of the way, and stumbled on, the pedestrian traffic parting and closing behind them without a ripple.

"A drug, I'll bet," Virgil guessed with a glance over his shoulder.

Molly agreed. "Like that kid wanted, back at the TT."

Diego didn't ask.

He paused at the curb, waited for something that looked like a junk pile sputter past, then hustled them across, just in time to see the junk pile round the corner and not quite make it to the upper lane. It skidded off the top of a coffeepot hovering at the intersection, veered sharply toward the pavement, veered sharply toward the "Memphis Belle," and finally sput-

tered over the heads of some people standing at the curb before bouncing once on the ground and rebounding into the air
where, with a squeal of air vents, it sputtered into its proper
lane and moved off.

But not before, in the bouncing and rebounding, it had hit
someone.

Diego saw it all—the sideswipe of the man in an ill-fitting
dark blue suit, the man spinning into another man wearing
dark green fur with just a daring touch of baubles, then spinning into a woman wearing dark brown skin. He eventually
hit a twisted green lamppost and flopped to the ground, shook
his head, grinned stupidly at those who attempted to help him,
then snarled at something, leapt to his feet, picked his left arm
off the ground and, waving it angrily over his head, charged
up the hill after the junk pile that had struck him.

Diego, not sure he had seen what he thought he had seen,
paused as they passed the queue where the man had landed, and
a young girl smiled up at him. "Cheap, y'know?"

He didn't know, and could barely think, but he assumed the
practiced expression of someone who did know until someone
else told him so he would know and not feel quite so dumb.

She nodded her agreement. "One of these days, the pearls
are going to put a stop to that." She shrugged as the others
agreed. "What can you do, huh? People gonna pay for it, people gonna find it."

Now that particular universal truth Diego understood, and
he grunted politely as he moved on.

Stopped.

Turned.

Stared at the young girl.

He had a sudden and distressing feeling she hadn't been
talking about the flying junk pile.

"Hey," Molly called from a few yards up the hill. "C'mon,
we don't have all day."

He didn't want to know.

"Moll," Virgil said, "you aren't going to believe what they
got in here."

He had to know.

"Virgil, for god's sake, move, okay? We don't have any
time to . . . my . . . god!"

He walked back to the young girl, who turned as if expecting him, and greeted him with a broad friendly smile. "You're a tour, right?"

He cleared his throat noncommittally.

The others in the queue, most of them relatively normal except for the guy in the armadillo suit—and he sincerely hoped it was an armadillo suit—studiously turned away with that nonchalant attitude all eavesdroppers have when they don't want anyone to know they're being nosy.

The girl, who at closer range wasn't nearly as young as Diego had first thought, and was most definitely a woman, touched his arm to move him closer. "Sorry," she said with a nod to the queue, "but I don't want to lose my place. I've been waiting hours for the damn bus. Could've been home by now."

He nodded knowingly.

She looked him over. Slowly. Carefully.

Very carefully.

She wore old-fashioned simple jeans, a simple pale blue blouse with stiffly pleated sleeves that looked sharp enough to slice stone, a simple silver band around her head, her blonde hair in a simple ponytail, and her feet were covered in simple rhinestone snakeskin boots complete with the snake's head and fangs at the toes, and spiked rattle heels high enough to bring her eyes damn near even with his.

Her face, when she widened her already friendly smile, was highlighted by a rounded dimpled chin and the greenest eyes he'd ever seen this side of an emerald necklace.

"Tour," she repeated.

He frowned his bemusement.

Her smile fell lopsided. "What I mean is, y'all are not from around here, right? Visiting? Vacationing? Trying to break into the biz?"

He nodded, even though he had no idea what "the biz" was.

She nodded.

"Them green folks up there your friends?"

He nodded, but only after a moment's consideration and strong temptation.

She lowered her voice as she leaned closer and nearly tipped over. "Do me a favor, tell them they gotta lose that green stuff, okay? Stand out like a whacked wing, you know? Picker can spot 'em a mile away, steal 'em blind."

Diego glanced toward his friends.

"Like your outfit, though."

"Thanks."

She stepped back and gave him the twice-over. "Fact is, I can see by your outfit that you are a cowboy."

He tilted his head in a noncommittal shrug. "Well, Miss, I can see by your outfit that you're a . . ." He stopped. He considered. He finished, "Lady."

One of the men in the queue snickered.

The woman glowered.

Diego had a feeling.

The feeling, however, went unexplored, unlabeled, and unexplained, because at that moment the still-snickering man stepped out of the line and said, "Hey, *lady*, you want to see me home?"

The eavesdroppers nearly broke their necks not listening.

"The name, mule," she answered tightly, "is Belle."

The man laughed. "Who cares?" He grabbed the crotch of his pale grey suit with dark blue stitching around the lapels and up the inseams, and waggled his hand in a most obscene and provocative manner. "So. You wanna ring my chimes or what?"

Diego didn't have time to find out what Belle's answer would have been; nor did he have time to see how far down the man's throat his fist would go.

Just as she opened her mouth to retort, someone shrieked, "Oh my Lord, preserve us and send us home in that golden chariot with the diamond wheels . . . it's *him*!"

And all hell, a couple of windows, and a few of the signs, broke loose.

CHAPTER 2

Diego had heard that kind of ominous commotion on several previous occasions, but before he could summon a specific memory in order that he might focus more clearly upon the causes and probable effects so that he could figure out what might be the proper response, the woman named Belle clamped on to his elbow and began hustling him up the block, doing her best to appear as if she was only removing herself prudently from a potentially dangerous situation rather than escaping from one.

Behind them, the queue had fragmented into several unruly factions, each of them staring, pointing every which way, yelling, shouting, and pointing some more, while more than a few clasped their hands and dropped to their knees right there on the boulevard, causing all manner of vehicular maneuvers—primarily up and away—necessary to avoid smearing their abrupt explosions of piety into the gutters.

For a moment Diego thought he heard a heavenly choir rise above the rising din.

Then he did hear a heavenly choir; a little heavy on the sopranos, but heavenly nonetheless.

Despite Belle's increasingly frantic insistence, he stopped.

And there swept out of the sky which would have been dark if it hadn't been for all that light, a symbolically twelve-foot long, pure white vehicle dazzling in its brightness, nicely trimmed in gold and silver, with darkly tinted windows all around, and an amazing set of polished and diamond-embedded longhorn steer horns bolted between its lasso-shaped headlights; it was also the apparent source of the angelic voices that almost made him think of the preacher's wife.

The crowd hushed.

Someone said, "Lordy, it's the chariot itself."

The crowd hushed again.

Someone else said, "Do you think *he'll* come out?"

The crowd hushed, but speculated.

The white vehicle circled once over the fray. Then, with a sighing "Amen," landed gently on the street.

The hush deepened.

A trumpet sounded a tastefully muted fanfare.

Seconds later a side door hissed upward to provide dramatic exit for a brawny man in a blinding white suit tailored to his bulky specifications, with a virtually impossible mane of thick white hair brushed and pomped away from his high flushed forehead. His eyes were an amazingly clear blue; his face was granite touched by an artist.

The trumpets faded into the distance.

The silence thickened.

A middle-aged woman scurried under the immense reach of the horns and whispered something to the man in white.

"Say . . . *what*?"

She glanced furtively into the crowd and repeated her message.

"He . . . *what*?"

She nodded.

He took a breath deep enough to spread the gold piping on his lapels.

Bowing and damn near scraping, she backed away.

He snapped his fingers, called for a mule, and a small man threw himself to his knees without hesitation before him, thus providing an instant if somewhat quivering platform for the man in white to stand on. Which he did. Raised his hands over his head, widened his eyes, and cried, "You have seen it, my friends! You have heard it! The Time has come! The Poke has peaked! The Way is open!"

"What . . .?" Diego asked.

Belle shook her head quickly. "No time." She tugged him away. "Just follow me."

"I say, hear me, dear people and you hopeless heathens who know not the Way, the Trail, and the Chariot of the Archangel! I say, *hear me!*" the man in white bellowed in a voice deep enough to stir the liver and quiver a few loins. "The Reverend Hiram Bufoally speaketh the Cowpoke Truth, for it is written and joyously sung around the Poke's Sacred Midnight Campfire that all men—I say, *all* men—shall rise *up* against the blasphemous Infidel and *smite*—"

His platform moaned and collapsed.

The preacher subsequently, although not without trying gamely to avoid it, toppled heavily to the ground, and there arose from the crowd such a wailing and gnashing of teeth that half the dentists in Greater Tennessee began planning early retirement.

"Hold up a minute," Diego said, fascinated by the spectacle of the preacher being assisted to his feet by a half dozen smaller sweaty men and one panting woman, all of whom were hailing and praying and screaming out something about Poking thy neighbor before he Pokes you.

"No," Belle insisted.

"But—"

"For god's sake, mister, look at them!"

He did.

He was horrified.

And being as how he was a judicious man who had seen the birth of a potential lynch mob more than once, though never with him as its target, he didn't argue further. Instead, as he passed Virgil, who was gaping through the oval window of a tiny shop displaying multi-colored vulcanized items of a nature completely beyond Diego's ken, he hooked the bigger man's arm and dragged him along.

"What . . .?" Virgil asked.

"Trouble," was the terse reply.

"Molly!" the tall hefty young bald man bawled over his shoulder.

Molly poked her head out the door of the shop in question and said, "What?"

"Trouble!"

She asked no questions, only threw up her hands in an *I should have known it was too easy* manner and hurried to join the others.

By that time the street was fast in the process of being filled with shouting, yelling, pointing, praying, and angry people of all costume persuasions and, evidently, social strata, many of whom gathered around the impossibly coiffed preacher, who had found another kneeler and was once again bellowing and waving his arms over his head.

For one frozen moment, nothing happened.

Then, as querulous voices were raised to demand explanation why they were doing this nonsense instead of heading home to a decent meal and some sectarian poking of their own, a half-filled bottle spiraled from the midst of the crowd and smashed through the window of the "Memphis Belle," causing sparks and not a few flames to spray over the pavement.

In retaliation, a corpulent man in a rhinestone-studded butcher's apron raced out of the establishment and threw a spiked club at the man in the white suit.

He missed, but the assault on the cleric was all the well-dressed rabble needed.

As Diego glanced back, he saw a svelte woman hike up her fashionably ankle-length, split halfway to obscenity skirt, pull out what was clearly a long-barreled knobby weapon of some kind, and fire it at a bald man trying to climb one of the green lampposts dotting the length of the curb. There was a flash of blue light at the muzzle, a beam of stark white light that flared from the muzzle's blue light, and a smoking hole soon appeared in the back of her victim's neck.

Another outraged scream.

Someone pulled out another weapon, this one much more compact and less ostentatious, and burned the woman's hair off.

The choir began to sing from the depths of the longhorn chariot.

Another window shattered as a steel chair from inside a food shop took the easy way outside, said chair bouncing smartly into the knees of an adolescent wearing a tailored tartan sheet artfully draped over his shoulders and toppling him directly into the path of a vehicle which hadn't had time to swerve, hop, climb, or stop.

The kid didn't have time either; he was pretty much squished before he hit the ground.

Diego winced. "What the . . .?"

"No time, keep moving, honey, these damn heels are breaking my ankles," Belle gasped as she shouldered her way boldly through those determined to race in the opposite direction."

"How did this start?" Molly asked fearfully.

When no one answered, she stared at Diego.

He stared back.

"Jesus, the white Indian again?"

"Nope."

"Some addle-pated woman," Belle explained after a hasty introduction and an exchange of wary looks and cautious sartorial compliments. "You get them around here sometimes, always proclaiming the Second Coming of somebody or other. It gets folks all riled somehow."

"And there's always a riot?" Virgil asked after a hasty introduction.

Belle nodded, checked behind them, and picked up the pace. "Comes of having too many preachers and not enough religions, you know what I mean? Especially that son of a bitch Bufoally. He preaches what he calls the Hangin' Salvation Gospel, has a place over by the jungle, you can see his signs all over the damn city. Remind me to tell you about him sometime." She looked back again. "If we get out of this mess alive, that is."

As they reached the top of the rise, several whooping sirens overwhelmed the din caused by the shouting, yelling, praying, and by now fiercely battling mob, not to mention the choir and the trumpets. Diego looked up just in time to see four very long bullet-shaped black cars swoop soundlessly except for the sirens down out of the night, or day, their sides bulging with large white globes, small white globes, and a string of globes looped gracefully across each hood.

Pearls, Diego thought.

The Law.

At the same time, Molly demanded to know why anyone would want to hurt them, for crying out loud, they were only doing a little shopping, for god's sake; Virgil said he didn't know, ask Diego, and when she did, he said he didn't know exactly but Belle here appeared to know and had advised him to make himself scarce before something terrible happened.

"Like what?"

A small explosion blossomed fire and acrid smoke from the middle of the mob.

"Never mind."

The amazing thing was, despite the potential for grievous harm and a couple of late-night funerals, even more people arrived on the scene, pouring eagerly out of guitars and dulcimers and a low-rent harmonica with most of its windows popped out, pushing and shoving their clamorous way toward the action, babbling excitedly and waving exotic weapons in the air.

Luckily Diego and his companions were ignored as they pushed through the crowds and hurried down the far slope as fast as they could without actually running. Here, though the towers were just as high, the sign and shop lights were much dimmer where they existed at all, and the constant noise not nearly as pervasive. Except for the trumpet, which was beginning to sound a little battered.

"Where are we going?" Virgil asked fearfully.

"The river," Belle said.

"I can't swim."

Diego didn't much care where they were going as long as they got there in time for him to ask a couple of pertinent questions, one of which had to do with the preacher, another the man with the portable arm, and a third the reason why Belle had begun to take sideways glances at him, frowning, shaking her head, then concentrating on not falling off her boots.

Midway toward the river, which was fairly invisible at this point, a knot of white Indian ruffians, each with a chicken feather knotted in his hair and smoking grease smeared on his loincloth, swarmed around the corner, muttering ominously to themselves.

Diego braced himself.

The ruffians moved on.

Or would have had not one tried to break rudely through the quartet's line instead of going around. And when Diego instinctively grabbed his shoulder to guide him on his way, he looked up.

Oh no, please, Diego thought miserably at the ruffian's startled expression; Lord, can't You give me at least one break tonight?

Apparently not.

The ruffian's nearly toothless mouth opened.

His bloodshot eyes bulged.

His chicken feather went all a-quiver.

And when he regained control of lungs and lips, he shrieked, "Yo! Brethren, wait! Rein up! Look! It's *him*!" and dropped immediately to his knobby knees into a position of quivering penitence and ambivalent expectation of fairly soon Divine punishment. His friends whirled at the startled cry of visionary discovery, took one look at the object of their buddy's fearful reverence, and instantly threw their own bodies to the pavement and beseeched the thoroughly bewildered man in the black suit not to blow them too precipitously into the next kingdom since they were pretty much not yet ready to leave this one, no matter what the preacher said.

Diego gaped.

Belle grabbed his arm again and dragged him onward.

"What the hell was that all about?" Molly demanded.

One of the white Indian ruffians sprang to his feet, waved his yellowhead tomahawk, and screamed that he had seen for himself and without means of artificial aid, the Light, the Truth, and the genuine Trail of the Poke, hallelujah, son of a bitch. Almost immediately, given the speed sound travels through hissing gunfire and fiery explosions and sirens and shouting and screaming and yelling and praying, the mob that had been bent on bringing the district around the deserted railroad station to its metaphorical knees poured over the crest in a frenzy not nearly big enough to hold them all.

It was led by Hiram Bufoally.

In his left hand he waved a rope at the end of which was a complicated series of knots which, when all was said and done, ended in a noose.

"Run!" Belle cried, whooped, and fell off her heels.

Diego snatched her up as Molly and Virgil sprinted away down the hill into the darkness.

Belle thanked him, took his hand, and they ran after his friends until she whooped and fell again, this time bringing Diego with her.

He helped her up, she thanked him, grabbed his arm, and they ran on for several blocks more until one of her heels rattled and snapped. Before either one had a chance to whoop, they toppled into a curbside kiosk carrying all manner of privately printed material which, as Diego plucked it angrily

from his face and chest, seemed to concentrate mostly on how
to become rich and famous overnight by taking a ten-month
course in plucking and yodeling.

Belle helped him to his feet.

The mob spotted them and screamed as one, that being the
preacher in the now rumpled white suit with the noose; his
hair was okay, though.

Molly and Virgil had already vanished.

"We'll never make it," Diego said, gauging the distance between what he assumed was safety and himself, then himself
and what he knew damn well was the ruination of his new
clothes and, probably, most parts of his body, which wasn't
new at all and damn near irreplaceable.

Belle didn't waste her breath arguing. She faced the ad-
vancing mob, scowled, aimed, and kicked off her boots one at
a time, spearing one gent square in the chest and another in
a place that pretty much guaranteed a life without grandchil-
dren bouncing on his knee; then she darted into an alley between what looked like a tambourine and what was most
definitely a severely dented triangle. Diego, having few options and not many more choices, followed as swiftly as he
could given the darkness of the alley, the unseen litter that lit-
tered it and threatened his footing, and the fact that his side
was acting up again. He pressed a hand against it and hoped
that the dampness he felt was nothing more than sweat.

Otherwise, it was blood.

Suddenly Belle said, "Damn."

"What?" he whispered as the mob reached the mouth of the
alley.

"I turned into the wrong place."

"How bad is it?"

"It's a dead-end."

CHAPTER 3

"Virgil, where did they go?"

"I don't know. They were right behind us a minute ago, weren't they?"

"Well, I can't see them now, damnit. All I can see are all those nuts up there, and they're still coming this way."

"You think we ought to go back and find them?"

"Virgil. Honey. Take a good look at that mob, okay? Take a good look at those cop car things. How far do you think we'll get up there before someone remembers us?"

"But we can't just leave them. It isn't right."

"No kidding, but are you going to fight them all with your bare hands?"

"You have the butter knife."

"Virge, I know how you feel, but we only have about two minutes to make up our minds."

"Well why don't we just get hold of one of the cops and tell them the truth?"

"Sure. We'll tell the cops—*if* we get to them before that mob gets to us—that we're not really criminals, we're actually innocent visitors from the Past, trying to find a replacement timer chip for our Time-Traveling train so we can go back to the nineteenth century, drop off our friend, then go up to the twentieth century and go home."

"I see your point."

"One minute, Virgil. Are you sure you can't swim?"

"Why don't we just take that bridge over there?"

"Jesus, you ask a lot of questions for a man about to be torn limb from limb. Because they'll see us if we try to cross that bridge over there, that's why. Assuming we can get to the bridge in one piece in the first place."

"So why won't they see us when we're in the water?"

"Because we'll be underwater, you big dope."
"You got that right. We'll be drowning."

CHAPTER 4

Through the skillful use of his hands, and a couple of muttered apologies to Belle who inadvertently kept getting in his way, Diego quickly felt around the disgustingly slimy confines of the alley he couldn't see all that well and had to admit that they were indeed at a dead end, although he wished there was another way to put it. The back wall was smooth cold stone and too high to climb over without some sort of very tall assistance; and as far as he could tell, with more apologies to Belle, the side walls were without windows or doors, just more slime even more disgusting than the slime on the back wall.

The first contingent of the mob milled hesitantly around the mouth of the alley, apparently not sure if their prey was actually in there.

A pearl car hovered uncertainly above them, itself too wide to enter without scraping the doors off.

A muffled explosion echoed in the distance.

This time, Diego allowed himself a relatively brief memory of the time he had been trapped in a boulder-packed box canyon by a gang of train robbers who had, coincidentally enough, just robbed a train as he had ridden into town in order to help stop them from robbing any more trains. Unfortunately, now that he permitted even more of the memory to surface, the similarities between that event and this one ended right there. He had only been trapped in the box canyon for a couple of hours because the posse he'd been leading had arrived just as the gang had figured Diego had run out of ammunition and was about to charge him. They were right. All he had left was a damn big pile of rocks which, he had hoped, would plunk a few out of their saddles before the rest of them got to him and plunked him out of his boots.

Belle, standing close behind as he turned resignedly to face the mob, whispered, "Sorry."

"It's all right."

"I was just trying to help."

"I know."

"They're going to tear us apart, unless Bufoally convinces them to let him hang us."

He shrugged fatalistically. It was bound to happen sooner or later, and although he would have much preferred it later, like about three hundred years or so in the Past, he wasn't about to quibble over the method his pursuers would finally choose. On the other hand, he wasn't about to let them come in and do as they pleased.

He straightened, spread his legs a little, took a slow deep breath, and swept his black coat away from his holsters.

"You can't kill them all," Belle gasped.

"Nope. Just enough to make 'em sorry."

The mob milled; the pearl hovered.

She pressed closer. "Maybe they'll miss us. It's awfully dark."

He didn't answer. Until he had judged the alley to be no more than five or six feet wide, and the mob at maybe a hundred, he had considered the same thing. But there was no convenient niche to duck into, no way they could ease around those who came in first.

He flexed his fingers.

He adjusted his hat.

"You know," she whispered as she released his arm, "I don't even know your name."

He watched the first few men step timidly into the alley, whispering to each other, nudging, and generally refusing to be the first to volunteer unless someone else volunteered at the same time.

"Please?"

He watched the pearl lift a little higher.

"Mister? Mister, please ... who are you?"

He felt a comforting calm settle over him, felt himself focus on the men who jostled each other as they crept closer,

ever closer, felt the world slip away as it always did whenever
he girded himself for battle.

Belle whispered, "Mister?"

He nodded.

Once.

CHAPTER 5

"They call me ... Diego."

CHAPTER 6

"Virgil, something's the matter with this water."

"Jesus, Moll, this is no time to bitch about it being too
cold, for god's sake."

"It isn't cold."

"Then what's the matter?"

"It's ... hard."

"What?"

"I'm standing on the water, Virge."

"Virgil."

"And there's something else."

"What now?"

"It's eating through my boots."

CHAPTER 7

In the uneasy silence that had fallen over the hesitant mob, the distant scream was fairly easy to hear, carrying as it did on the breeze that had fortuitously except for the screamer sprung up at that time. One would be hard-pressed to say whether the screamer was male or female, but evidently the mob didn't care. As the hovering pearl car abruptly whined, backfired, and swerved toward the river, Hiram Bufoally waved his holy noose in the air and lumbered off at full speed. The mob followed suit, trumping the scream with one of its own. Within seconds, the alley was free of the lethal menace which had, only seconds before, menaced it, and all that was left was Diego, trying to find out if he had lost his hearing.

For in the dim light that filtered in from the street, he could see that Belle's mouth was open. Wide. In the unmistakable gulp-and-hitch attitude of one who had every intention of screaming as soon as her lungs stopped filling with enough air to make that scream loud enough to deafen him, bring back the mob and, in the process, perhaps bring the alley walls down on his head.

When he realized that the mysterious scream just heard in the distance wasn't going to be anywhere near like the scream he was about to hear if he didn't act soon, he clamped his hand over her mouth, his arm around her shoulders, and hugged her snugly to his side as he hustled her back to the alley's mouth. Along the way, he realized that without those deadly boots of hers, the top of her head barely reached the center of his chest. So how, he wondered as he was forced to tighten his grip, can someone so tiny be so damn strong?

The future, he decided, has a lot of explaining to do.

Once at the entrance, and having gotten the hang of

avoiding most of the kicks her bare but powerful feet tried to
plant inside his shins, he peered warily around the corner and
saw a few dozen stragglers huffing their way toward the bottom of the slope, as the four pearl cars whooshed and sirened
impressively above them, eye-watering spotlights darting
from their roofs at virtually every angle but down. In the opposite direction, the broad boulevard was deserted save for a
few of the mildly injured, moaning and groaning to no visible
effect since there wasn't anyone around to assist them.

He had but a few heartbeats to decide.

He decided.

Without removing either hand or arm, and doing his best to
avoid those sharp-looking pleats on her sleeves, he half carried, half walked Belle to the other side of the street, returned
to the top of the hill and turned right, into a street similar to
the one just left in that it was pretty much a wreck from all
the rioting. Even the moving pictorial and word signs had
fallen silent, and still, although the neon still buzzed now and
then. This too was a downhill avenue, though not half as
steep nor half as wide as the one the mob had taken. It was,
however, in extremely poor repair, and halfway to the next
block and tired of dodging potholes even in the sidewalk, he
ducked into the doorway of a ukelele and allowed himself a
chance to rest.

Belle began to struggle anew.

Another decision had to be made.

He made it.

He turned her face toward him and said, "If I take my hand
away, are you going to scream?"

Her wide, terrified, but exceedingly beautiful green eyes
told him *damn right.*

Diego, even though he had been sorely provoked at times,
had seldom had the unpleasant opportunity or motive to either hit or shoot a woman. Not that they wouldn't hit or
shoot back, because they had, a number of times; yet there
remained within him something that balked at taking such
drastic measures against the opposite sex. Nevertheless, considering the circumstances of his still being in danger of losing his life in a future he never would have reached had he
been lucky enough to die in his own lifetime, he deepened
his voice and said:

"Belle, pay close attention. I'm going to have to pop you one if you scream, you understand? I ain't going to like doing it, but you know a couple of things I don't, and I want to know what they are before those idiots come back and string me up. Which they will do if you scream."

Her eyelashes batted the hell out of the still night air.

"I give you my word—if you keep quiet, I won't hurt you."

He felt her lips moving softly against his palm, a not unpleasant sensation, but entirely inappropriate to the situation at hand.

"Well?"

As he waited, he could sense the debate raging within her, could see the indecision wrestling with the fear in her expression, could almost feel the tug-of-war between her desire to bring rescue and her virtually visible desire to believe him, not to mention the other kind of desire which, like the lips, was not precisely what he had in mind. At least not for now, anyway. He was, after all, only human, and it had, after all, been a long time.

Three hundred years, to be exact.

Give or take.

Then he saw in those deep emerald eyes the wrong side winning the internal debate.

"Let me put it another way," he told her flatly. "You scream, and I promise you, it'll be the last sound you'll ever make."

She stiffened.

He hoped she believed him.

She glared.

He weighed his chances and decided there was nothing else to do—either she kept quiet and lived, or she screamed and he'd have to decide what to do then since, if she screamed and he made good on his threat, it would be the first time a woman would have died at his hand. It wasn't a pleasant thought. Except maybe for that overweight virago in Mexico City, who had pinned him under her considerable tonnage until he agreed to marry her and take her with him back to the United States. Since he didn't even know her name, had never seen her before, and had, before she sat on him, been only taking an afternoon's libation in a local cantina, he refused. She had shifted. He had struggled for air. She had snarled. He had turned blue. The bartender clunked her with a skillet and she had toppled hard enough to raise enough dust to allow him to escape. Crawling, to be sure, but in the right direction.

Belle, however, wasn't a virago.

Besides, she had taken to licking his palm.

All right, he told her with a look; it's your move.

Slowly, very slowly, he lowered his hand and slid his arm from around her shoulders.

Slowly, very slowly, she backed away until the canted wall of the recessed entrance stopped her. She licked her lips nervously. Her hands clasped white-knuckled in front of her before sweeping up and back through her hair, then down to her sides where she patted her legs as she thought.

Diego waited.

And then she said, "Between the eyes."

Had there been a harmonica player in the immediate vicinity, the effect her statement had on him would have been greatly enhanced.

As it was, someone down the street sneezed.

"Between the eyes," she repeated.

"I ..." He stared in disbelief. "What?"

Her lips began an uncontrollable quivering which she quelled only by wiping the back of her hand hard across her mouth several times. "If you shoot me ..." She swallowed hard and tried again. "If you shoot me, you'll shoot me between the eyes, won't you?"

He couldn't help stepping back himself. "Well, hell, how did you know that?"

She didn't answer. She sagged instead, braced herself against the wall, and shook her head in wonder. "I don't believe it. I just do not believe it." She looked out at the gleaming, neon-stained, garishly dismally bleak street with the litter blowing listlessly ahead of the breeze. "You hear that? You hear what I'm saying?" After a short bitter laugh, she looked back at him, frowning intently. "Y'all are pulling my leg, aren't you?" She shook her head once. "No. You're not." She leaned toward him. "Are you?" She leaned away. "No. Well, maybe. Who the hell knows?" She leaned toward him. "You shining or something?" She shook her head and leaned away.

"No. Don't look like it. You can't be." Close again, and a penetrating stare. "Nope. You're not the type." She leaned away. "Now how the hell do I know that?"

She leaned forward, frowning again, and he grabbed her arms, held her still, and waited until the vertigo passed and he could see straight again.

"Belle," he said, "would you mind telling me just what in the hell you're talking about?"

When she opened her mouth to scream, he dropped his hands hastily, and braced for another decision; when she collapsed against the wall without making a sound except for a tiny frustrated gurgle, he clamped his hands against his thighs to keep his fingers from doing what they'd been trained to do and were getting cramps from not doing; when she reached into her blouse and pulled out a small silver locket in the shape of what couldn't possibly be a Diego Special, it must be the light, and thumbed it open, all he could do was wait patiently.

She pointed at him. "Diego."

He nodded.

She pointed at the ivory-handled guns in his holsters. "Specials."

He nodded, and refused to give in to the abrupt sinking feeling that brought his stomach down around the level of his knees. He had already been through this unsettling bout of incredulous, *Lord I must be dreaming I thought he was dead by now*, recognition with Virgil and Molly back when he had first entered the Time Thing; but to think that it would happen here as well was something he did not, under any conditions, want to contemplate, even if it already had and there wasn't much he could do about it but wait for the sequence to play itself out.

Meanwhile, Belle pulled her ponytail over her shoulder and across her mouth, and bit down thoughtfully on as much of it as she could squeeze between her lips. Then she sidled closer to the sidewalk, crooked her finger at him, and pointed at the locket. He looked over her shoulder, and saw a tiny black-and-white photograph nestled ever so cleverly inside the cylinder. He leaned closer, his chin digging into her shoulder, and looked again.

"Damn," he said.

• • •

It was him.

It was, by all the rules of life that he had ever learned and a few that he'd made up along the way to cover the ground for which there had previously been no rules, impossible. While it was true that he had, once or twice, allowed himself to be talked into posing for his photographic portrait, it was beyond the realm of possibility that Belle Whatshername from Nashville several centuries later had somehow managed to find a picture of him small enough to place in a silver locket just like one of his Diego Specials.

He looked again.

It was still him.

She said something.

He couldn't understand and told her so.

She whirled, pointed angrily at his chest just shy of poking a hole in it, and said it again.

He reached out and gently removed the ponytail from her mouth.

"You stupid, mule-head son of a bitch!" she sputtered, cheeks reddening, eyes narrowed, forehead furrowing, dimpled chin jutting. "What do y'all think you're doing?" She took a furious step toward him. "You know what they'll do to you if they catch you? Do you have any idea what in the name of what-all they'll do when they find you?"

Somewhere among all those heated questions was an important nugget of interpretive information, but he'd be damned if he knew what it was. She was making about as much sense as Molly had when she had tried to explain the twentieth century.

"Now look," he began.

"No!" She slammed her hands on her hips and raised her dimpled chin. "You look, mister. You come sashaying in here wearing those clothes and looking like you do, what did you expect those people out there to do—fall down and kiss your goddamn feet?"

Diego drew himself up. "No," he said. "Couple of them tried, but that wasn't my doing."

Her arms flapped at the air. "Jesus. You are a piece of something, you know that?" She scowled. "Are you really that thick?"

His expression hardened.

Immediately she realized her error and passed a calming palm lightly over her face. Then she inhaled slowly and deeply several times. "Look, it's real easy, mister—you can't go around town looking like that, it's that simple. We're going to have to do something, I don't know what, or they'll hang you sure as we're standing here."

"Then let's not stand here," he told her, took her arm, and brought her to the sidewalk, turning downhill.

Not ten paces later he stopped, turned around, and brought her back to the doorway.

"What?" she asked.

He shook his head. "I can't go. My friends."

"Mister—"

"Diego."

She groaned. "Now damnit, what in the world did I just tell you?"

"It's my name."

"Right. I know. They call you . . . Diego."

He thought for a second, then shrugged. "I don't know. Somehow it doesn't sound quite the same. Something's missing."

She took hold of his arm.

He resisted, reminding her sternly that he wasn't about to desert his friends.

She reminded him that a couple of hundred awfully mad people and who knew how many pearls were probably, at this very moment, trying to fit the pieces of his friends together so they could see what they had just torn apart with their bare hands. Unless Reverend Bufoally and his people had gotten there first, in which case they were watching his friends turn in the wind as they hung from the limb of some twisted old tree on the banks of the Tennessee River.

He suggested tightly that it was a hell of a way for a town to treat someone just because they wore godawful green underwear, and besides, she couldn't be sure that's what had really happened. It was, he added before she could get in another lick, entirely possible that his friends had managed to escape and were even now hiding somewhere, waiting for him to come get them.

She doubted it.

He knew his friends better than she did.

She supposed he did, but he wasn't going to get two feet trying to locate them wearing those clothes.

These clothes, he snapped, had been worn through worse scrapes than this and hadn't done him any harm.

She admitted, at second, third, and fourth extensive glances, that the black suit with the extra-long jacket to cover the tooled holsters, the silver-threaded vest, the ruffled shirt, and the hat with the bullet hole in the low flat crown did look more than passably good on his frame, but the people who were going to kill him wouldn't much care how he looked dressed as long as he looked dead.

He told her rather impatiently that they were wasting valuable time discussing his choice of outfits, and if she had any ideas, he'd be obliged if she spat them out now before they both died of old age.

She leaned out of the doorway and gazed thoughtfully down the brightly lit street, and at the pedestrians popping in and out of the shops along the way. Her bare foot tapped. She sniffed. She gnawed a little on her ponytail.

"Okay. I got it."

"What do you got?"

Without a word she snatched off his hat. When he snarled and grabbed for it, she set it on her own head, took it off, took off her silver headband, put the hat back on, turned him around and mangled his hair into a semblance of a ponytail, turned him back and shook her head in mild despair. "It isn't much of a disguise, you going bare-headed and all, and ponytails aren't your style, you know what I mean? but if you take off that jacket and kind of sling it over your shoulder, carefree like, maybe we'll get there without any trouble."

"Get where?" he asked as he slung the jacket carefree like over his shoulder.

"A place where you can get just about anything you want, long as you got the notes to pay for it."

Amazing, he thought; some things just don't change.

On the other hand, one thing would definitely change once this was over—his ponytail. He felt like a jackass, and probably looked like one too. Although, he thought further when he glanced into a shop window, that silver band added a nice touch; kind of matched his vest and gunbelt studs.

"So where is this place? I haven't got all night. Neither do my friends."

"Not far. A couple of blocks, that's all." She grinned up at him. "We'll be there before you know it."

"If I knew it," he grumbled, "I wouldn't be here in the first place."

"But if you weren't here, you wouldn't have met me."

She winked.

He winked back without thinking, realized what he had done, winked with the other eye to cancel the first wink, then winked both eyes just to be on the safe side and thought he had gone suddenly blind until she put an elbow in his gut and told him to stop horsing around, this was serious business here in case he hadn't noticed.

He had.

He told her so.

Then he asked her why in hell he had to change clothes anyway.

"Honey," she drawled as she tugged him out of the doorway, "you go around Nashville dressed like the Poke, you're asking for trouble."

"Didn't ask for it, got it anyway. Who the hell is the Poke?"

She frowned. "You . . . I'll be damned. You really don't know, do you?"

A pearl siren wailed over the rooftops.

"Nope," he said.

A young man stumbled past them, his face streaked with dried blood.

She kept them close to the buildings, averting her own face whenever a car flew by.

"The Poke," he reminded her. "Who or what is he?"

She looked up at him and said, "God, honey. Bless your little heathen heart, you're dressed just like God."

CHAPTER 8

Molly huddled miserably against the twisted rusted hulk of some metal contraption discarded high on the stained pink concrete shore of the hardwater river that wound through and around the city. She was cold, though the air was warm, and she hugged herself tightly as she waited for Virgil to finish scouting the area to see if the mob and the pearls had really given up the chase. Far above her, the glittering towers of Nashville poked their unique way into the sky, great patches of darkness alternating irregularly with great patches of winking light. Once in a while something flew past soundlessly, darting between the buildings like a firefly in search of a little fun before dawn. Oddly enough, on the other side of the river it was completely dark, as if nothing, or no one, lived over there.

In fact, if she stared long enough, she could swear all that dark was the surface of a wall.

She shifted, froze when her boot dislodged a pebble and sent it rattling down the rough-surface slope toward the river, and not until a full minute's silence had passed did she allow herself to breathe again.

Where the hell is he? she wondered, anxiety and anger boiling acid in her stomach. Not that she didn't appreciate his volunteering for the job, but it was his own damn scream after all that had brought all those people after them again. As they sprinted away, he had tried to explain that he had seen *something* rising out of the water behind her, but since the river's surface was about as hard as the cement she crouched on now, all she could do was curse a little, run a lot, and finally drag him behind this . . . whatever it was, until the danger passed.

Which it did.

Remarkably quickly.

Curiously enough, there was no intensive search along the riverbank, no swooping of glaring spotlights across the carcasses of any of the other rusted and discarded metal things scattered along the riverbank, no bullhorns demanding they surrender immediately and come out with their hands up, no search parties, no peasants with torches.

Once it was clear they weren't where they were when Virgil had screamed, the man in the white suit left, the mob broke up, and the pearls flew away.

Just like that.

Now she could only hope that Diego would find them, or Virgil would find Diego and the two of them would find her, so they could all make their way back to the Time Thing, rest for a while, then figure out another way to get that timer chip so they could finally go home, take a bath, have a good laugh over their adventure, and, if she had her way, take that damn train apart, piece by piece.

She shivered.

She didn't much like the future, and it was hell on her boots.

It was hell on her lungs, too, when something tapped her shoulder and she shrieked and was halfway to the river before an arm scooped her off her feet and swung her back to the safety of whatever it was she'd been hiding behind.

"Hush!" Virgil warned.

She scrambled for the butter knife.

He grinned. "You'll never guess what I did. Not in a million years."

Failing to find the butter knife spurred her on to see how many holes she could gouge in his smug little face with her nails, which, somehow, he managed to avoid simply by clamping his hands around her wrists.

"Go ahead," he said. "Guess."

"You have five seconds to live."

"Nope. Guess again."

Her adrenaline sighed back into place, her limbs relaxed, and she shook her head sorrowfully. "Y'know, for someone who's invented Time Travel, *and* traveled through Time, *and* has met his boyhood hero, *and* has actually taken his Driver and his boyhood hero into the unknown Future, you sure can be damn dumb sometimes."

"Nope," he said agreeably. "Last chance."

Killing him wouldn't do, she decided. Even though she was the Driver, he was the only one who knew how to start the Theoretical Time Displacement engine. All she had to do was steer. Which, while in and of itself was no small feat since she was the only person on the face of the Earth—or anywhere else, for that matter—who could do it, the entire process was a two-person job.

Or, one woman and a big green dope.

A big, green, bald dope.

He held his hands behind his back, then presented them, closed, to her. "Pick."

"Virgil, don't you think—"

"Pick."

She slapped the left one.

He opened the hand, palm up.

She looked at the palm.

She looked at him.

She said, "I'm speechless."

Smugly he settled on the ground and dropped the timer chip back into his breast pocket before bracing his hands behind him. "It was easy. I was looking around for Diego, kind of sneaking and all, and pretty soon I saw I was near that store. There wasn't anybody around but some guy playing some pretty mean air guitar on the corner, so I walked in, asked for the chip, the guy gave me one and I walked out." He shrugged. "Southern hospitality, I guess."

"What did you have in your other hand?" she said.

He shrugged again. "Just this metal bar thing I found in the gutter. I threw it away later."

Molly grinned, scowled, giggled, frowned, and finally hugged him. She knew Virgil would never have actually threatened the man, but she also knew that he had had lots of practice in silent intimidation, working as he had done for his father, whose entire life had been spent developing a successful if small-time working relationship with shopkeepers and local politicians who didn't want their knees broken over something as trivial as missing a protection payment. Virgil never did the actual breaking; that was someone else's job.

What Virgil did was loom.

And as far as she could tell, he loomed just about better

than anyone else in New York City who wasn't doing five-to-ten in the federal pen.

It seemed to work pretty well in Nashville, too.

"So now what do we do?" he said.

"How about going back to the TT and fixing it so we can make a quick getaway?"

"But what about Diego?"

"C'mon, Virge, he's—"

"Virgil."

"—a smart man. He'll know enough to go to the TT just in case we made it back. And when he shows up, it's pedal to the metal and here we come, nineteen ninety—"

"Eighteen."

"What?"

"Eighteen. We have to bring Diego back to eighteen-eighty, remember?"

"Oh. Yeah."

He looked at her, smiled knowingly, and brushed a hand gently over her hair. "I'll miss him, too, Moll, but we have to do what's right."

"I know, I know." She kissed him quickly on the cheek and pushed herself to her feet. "So let's get going before he starts another riot."

Virgil laughed as he stood. "I wonder what that was all about, anyway?"

"Virgil."

"Y'know, you'd think he was a wanted criminal or something, his picture in all the post offices. Hey."

"Virge?"

"I wonder if they still have post offices anymore."

"Virgil!"

"What?"

"Remember that thing you said you screamed at that I didn't believe you about?"

Virgil looked at the river.

He didn't scream.

Neither did Molly.

Terror sometimes does that to intrepid Time Travelers.

PART III

The Magnificent Six,

and an Idiot

CHAPTER 1

The current problem, in a kind of tactical sense, was that when Diego's jacket was hung carefree like over his shoulder, his six-guns were exposed to all who bothered to notice them. And despite the fact that the citizenry of whatever century he was in, he was beginning to lose track, seemed to possess weapons not even his nightmares could conjure, it was apparently still not proper to have those weapons in full view of the people against whom those weapons were going to be used, probably. Therefore, before an alarm was raised and the pearls showed up again, Belle slipped her arm around his waist, thus effectively covering the left, or emergency, revolver, while Diego himself dangled his right arm casually along his side in order to minimize possible discovery of the right one. At the same time, they stayed as close to the buildings as possible, without actually falling through any of the entrances.

The pedestrians didn't seem to notice anything; they were too busy swarming in small numbers from one side of the street to the other, popping in and out of shops and offices, and generally not much giving a damn. About anything.

Not that Diego cared anyway. He was too busy thinking about all Belle had just told him after telling him he looked like God. Which, as it turned out and much to his relief, was something of an exaggeration.

He was not, strictly speaking, a church-going man. All that hot air trapped in an equally hot building was not to his liking. Whenever he felt the need to check, he thought that riding across the prairie in spring did the job just fine. And while folks sometimes mistook him for someone else of their brief acquaintance, there wasn't anyone that he could recall who considered him in any way godlike.

In fact, to a fair segment of the population he was aware of, the reaction was often quite the opposite.

But that was then, and this was whenever the hell it was, and as Belle guided him around a corner and down another gentle slope, he wondered how in the name of four steers named Bill the country had lasted as long as it had.

Which, when he thought about what Belle had said, it hadn't. Sort of. Vaguely.

Apparently, after the South rose again, took a clear look around and hated what it saw, various sections of North America took their own looks around, hated what they saw, put their hats on and went home. The result was places like Greater Tennessee, Lesser Des Moines, Large Yukon and its affiliates in Quebec, and a scattering of Minor This's and Not So Hot Thats. Confusion lasted for nearly a century, until the automobilelike flyers were developed on MoonBase Tranquility and exported to Mother Earth. Travel resumed with a vengeance. Cultures clashed. Politicians clashed. Religions clashed. Europe clashed, but nobody paid any attention.

And when things eventually settled down, the smoke cleared, and the Bulgarians bought and sold just about everything they could get their hands on and went home, and it was evident that population exchanges between the Lessers and the Greaters and the Minors also included contemporary technology, which itself included fascinating if somewhat lethal new drugs, areas like Greater Tennessee once more found themselves on the crest of potential upheaval and unrest.

The black market flourished until the Indians took over and flooded the fruited plain with everything but oranges; local law enforcement agencies banded together into an almost competent continental information and cooperation network; the United Nations Space Exploration and Science Development Agency released its blueprints for cybernetic and android production into the capitalistic free market, which pretty much put the rubber doll industry clean out of business; Elvis died; and for the fourth time in three hundred years, Nashville became the Music Capital of the Universe, except on several Neptunian moons where water sports were the main attraction.

Thus it was that thousands of pilgrims arrived in Nashville by foot, flyer, and commuter monorocket every day, and thousands more left, their dreams, bank accounts, and air guitars crushed. But still they came, and still they left, and still they filled the bars and auditoriums and arenas and saloons, looking for that brass ring, that one moment of recognition, that one knowing smile that would make it all worthwhile.

When Diego expressed mild puzzlement—out of courtesy, actually, because he was completely baffled—Belle dragged him into an entertainment center, the centerpiece of which was a large room filled with tables and chairs, the chairs filled with people, the people watching a rhinestone-bedecked young man on a stage playing a guitar that, somehow, shimmered insubstantially. His lips were moving, but they made no sound. Neither did his back-up group, most of whom were yawning.

"Hologram," Belle explained as she plucked a long needle from the black wall. The needle was attached to a long black wire, which vanished into the wall. Diego noticed then that everyone in the place had one of those needles. He also noticed that the needles were jammed into their arms. He further noticed that Belle touched the tip of the needle to her forearm, winced, and returned the needle to its place.

"Cowboy song," she muttered. "Jesus." She pulled him out again. "I am sick to *here* with goddamn cowboy songs. No offense."

None was taken. He had been on trail drives before, and much preferred listening to a cow bawling for its lost calf. Cowboys who thought they could sing generally didn't make it through the night. Even if they remembered all the words. Which they usually didn't. And the ones they made up to fill in the gaps were usually foul enough to curl a cactus.

"You see, honey," she explained as she pulled him into yet another narrow street, yet again heading downward, "the cowboy songs are romantic, y'know? Wide open spaces, starry nights, sitting around the campfire? You know?"

He didn't know. That same trail drive was about as far from romance as he had been in years. The cattle smelled, the drovers smelled, the horses smelled, the air smelled, and the food was enough to turn a man to religion. The accommodations were spartan, dust and bugs vied for squatter's rights in a man's beard, and a bath was something you took when there was a downpour and the stupid cattle weren't stampeding. He reckoned, from the enraptured expressions on the faces of those in the audience, a few things had been lost in translation through the years.

But he could also see that this was, for some unknown reason, a thriving and lucrative business. Belle concurred and explained that it was only a matter of time before someone figured out how to exploit those thousands of souls searching for that one melody, that one lyric, that one strike to the heart chord that would make them rich, famous, and artistically justified.

That someone, these days, was the Reverend Hiram Bufoally.

No one knows where he came from.

One day he wasn't here and everything was rather peaceful in a honky-tonk, late Saturday night sitting on the porch with your momma sort of way; the next day he was here, standing four square on the river and preaching the Hangin' Salvation Gospel, which, evidently, was based upon an actual paper book he had discovered during a revelatory trip to New York City while in his callow youth with nothing better to do and lots of money to spend. The fact that the book was real paper and not imitation cauliflower would have been astounding in any free society where reading was something you did on signposts and wristbooks and computer screens small enough to fit on the inside of your eyeglasses; the information contained therein was absolutely astonishing.

Before long, the Reverend Bufoally had not only amassed a good-size fortune, he had also gathered around him a dedicated corps of followers who, if they had their Way, would plunge the entire continent back into the nineteenth century, thus purging itself of all manner of ill and bad habits. Thus begat the cowgirls, the white Indians, the Buffalo Herd, the mules who did all the shit work, and several other minor but related industries, all owned and operated by Hiram Bufoally.

Anybody who got in the way soon found that not even the prestigious Memphis Artificial Limb and CyDroid Laboratory Emporium could put them back together again.

"Why doesn't anyone stop him?" Diego asked in self-admitted foolish innocence.

"Because," Belle answered, "they're afraid he might be right. The Coming of the Poke and all that."

"What about those who don't believe him?"

"They look the other way. They figure, see, he'll fade just like all the others."

"You don't think he will."

"No."

"Why?"

She fingered the silver Special around her neck. "Because I used to be one of them."

She looked up at him.

He looked down at her.

She said, "I also saw the Book."

He looked away.

She looked away.

"Your picture's in it."

He looked down at her.

She looked up at him.

He said, "You're shi— pulling my leg."

She looked away.

He looked away.

She looked back.

"Three or four times in the past ten years, some guy's come riding into town, dressed like you, claiming to be the Cow-poke."

He looked back.

"They hanged 'em all. Right in front of that old railroad station. Unless they hanged them in the Arena."

He looked away, just in time to stop himself from colliding with a brick wall. By the time he'd regained his equilibrium, Belle had stopped them at the mouth of yet another alley. It wasn't as dark in there as it had been in the first alley; sputtering weak neon relieved most of the gloom if not the shadows, but it was clear this wasn't a place ordinary folks entered while strolling around town enjoying the sun, if, that is, the sun was out, which was still impossible to tell but they probably had ways of telling even if he didn't.

"That's why," she said softly, "we have to get you some new clothes."

"I like mine just fine."

"But damnit, mister, haven't you been listening? As far as

these people are concerned, you're a blasphemer! You look
too much like the Grand Poke!"

He stepped into the alley, saw an empty crate against the
slimy dripping damp warm wall, put on his jacket, took off
the headband and let his hair free, picked her up and set her
on the crate so he could look her square in the eyes. Then he
tilted his hat back on her head and looked her square in the
eyes.

"Little lady," he said as angrily as he could without actually being really angry, although he was getting there pretty
damn fast, "I *am* . . . Diego."

"Right. And I'm Belle Starr."

"Nice to meet you."

Her mouth opened.

He held up a warning finger.

Her mouth closed.

"Now," he said, "with all this explaining and telling going
on, seems that I ought to understand what's happening. I
don't. I didn't in New York. I don't now. So what we're going
to do is, we're going to this place you want to take me to,
we're going to find something to cover up what I'm wearing,
and then we're going back to the TT to wait for my friends."

Belle gestured with her forefinger, the gist of which was
permission to say something without him clamping her quiet
again.

He nodded.

"The TT?" she asked.

"Yep. It's what they call it. Means the Time Thing."

"Sugar," she said, "what in the name of all that's holy is a
Time Thing?"

He suspected possible trouble here, yet couldn't see his
way out of it. It seemed to be his Fate. Or a by-product of the
curse that old Sioux put on him up in Dakota just because
Diego had stepped on a sacred beetle whose spirit happened
to be the old man's dead wife.

Either way, he was getting pretty tired of it.

The beetle was damn ugly, too.

"It's a train."

"The Time Thing is a train."

"Sorta. Looks like a train, but it don't ride on tracks. Rides
on Time instead, the way I figure it."

She nodded thoughtfully, pulled her ponytail over her shoulder and stuffed it in her mouth.

He pulled it out when he couldn't understand her muttering.

She said, "You're trying to tell me you've been traveling through Time?"

"Don't know what else to call it."

"How about nuts?"

A not unreasonable description, he decided, all things considered and considering what he'd been through trying to get back home and ending up here instead.

She smiled sweetly.

He waited.

She said, "I'm not all that educated, you understand, but I do know that Time Travel is impossible. Which means you're nuts. Which explains why you're dressed the way you are." Her smile widened. Sweetly. "Which means—"

She bolted from the crate before he could stop her and raced down the alley, colliding with a shadow that stepped out of the shadows, knocking the shadow back into the shadows, and running on.

Diego wasted several precious seconds trying to decide if he should go after her, those seconds ending when he heard the faint wail of a pearl car somewhere in the city and realized that, while he might be able to find his way back to the station and the TT by himself, there was a pretty good chance he wouldn't be able to do it without being spotted by some fool white Indian or one of those quick-draw machete cowgirls. And if one of them spotted him, it would be a fair bet with a new deck that that pork-belly preacher and his damn white chariot wouldn't be too far behind.

With his noose.

He ran.

Stopped.

Reached down and gingerly took off his spurs, which were making entirely too much noise for someone trying to be inconspicuous, and slipped them into the special inside pockets he had had tailored into his new jacket which, he noted as he started running again, was looking pitifully old these days.

Besides, she had his new hat.

The crown and silver band of which he could see just

ahead, bobbing in and out of the light spilling from doorways
and, overhead, high narrow windows. As he dodged puddles
and pools of liquids he was fairly positive hadn't yet been
discovered by any scientist he ever heard of, he noticed that
Belle wasn't actually running very fast. In fact, she was pretty
much skipping, mostly side to side, her arms flapping, her
knees high, and her ponytail whacking her a good one in the
chops every few steps.

He caught up with her in no time, opposite a shop whose
sign indicated that pleasures unbounded—or not, depending
on your taste—could be found within for a very reasonable
price. There were no artistic interpretations of the wares as
there had been on the main street, but he figured the naked
woman standing on the milking stool just over the threshold
would give anyone a fair idea of what to expect.

He grabbed Belle's arm, and nearly cried out in surprise
when she leapt into his arms and wrapped her arms around
his neck and her legs around his thighs. Tightly. He nearly
toppled until he snared her around the waist, the maneuver
turning him to face the woman on the stool over Belle's
shoulder.

"Belle," the woman said dryly, "that ain't very seemly."
She smiled at Diego. "Anna. Anna Whiplash." She nuzzled
the bullwhip snuggled around her neck. "Any friend of
Belle's is a friend of mine."

Diego, not sure how to respond, nodded a greeting.

Belle leaned back and said, "Boots."

He adjusted his grip and said, "What?"

"You have boots on. I don't. Jesus, this place is dis*gust*-
ing."

From another establishment farther along the alley came
the discordant blare of an orchestral finale. Anna cursed,
hopped off the stool, waved goodbye, and vanished into the
depths of what Diego figured was the boldest bordello he had
ever seen outside Minneapolis, where they usually dressed in
furs and weren't much fun to look at up there in the red-
lighted window. A heartbeat later, another woman took her
place, this one wearing a loincloth, plastic gloves up to her elbows, and the longest, reddest snake he had ever seen in his
life.

"Belle honey," the snake woman chided wearily, "that ain't the way to do it."

"Shut up, Zannylee," Belle muttered.

The second naked woman reached into the snake's mouth, twisted her arm sharply, and when the hand came out again, the serpent began writhing clumsily across her breasts and shoulders. It would have been incredible if it hadn't been for the purple sparks occasionally darting from one of the eyes.

Belle shifted then, and Diego was forced to turn in a slow awkward circle to keep his balance. When he stopped, he watched a man stumble out of a green-lined door on the other side of the alley. He wore scuffed boots, jeans, a plaid shirt, and a bandanna, and smacked twice into the jamb before making it completely outside. When he looked up, Diego saw his eyes—they glowed. Brighter when he peered myopically around Diego's shoulder and said, "Hey, Zannylee, you got a minute for an old friend, huh?"

The snake woman snorted.

The shiner grinned stupidly and made his way toward her, slipping only once on a puddle of disgusting semi-liquid before falling out of sight.

"Second thought," Zannylee said to Belle, "maybe you got the right idea."

"Move," Belle whispered then.

Diego moved.

"Not that way," she snapped, and jerked her head toward the alley's darker regions. "That way."

He moved.

And as he did he noted several disconcerting things: that Belle wasn't nearly as heavy as she had been when first she'd leapt so nimbly into his arms; that she was the first woman he had held in his arms in far too long; that she wasn't struggling at all anymore; that her head lay on his shoulder; that she smelled kind of like spring in the high desert; and that he was noticing entirely too much about entirely too many parts of her for his own peace of mind.

He also noticed that, although the alley wasn't deserted by any means, few of the establishments he passed had names, signs, or other indications of their no doubt dubious stock in trade. It seemed that you came here knowing exactly what you wanted and where to get it; not, he remembered, unlike

certain areas of San Francisco, except for the awful bubbling
stuff seeping from under the alley walls.

Then Belle said, "Stop."

He stopped.

She raised her head from his shoulder and looked at him as
best she could considering they were nearly touching noses.
Diego, for his part, simply squinted.

"Those women back there," she said.

He waited.

"They're kind of . . . they sort of . . . I sometimes . . . they
know what I . . . I never really actually . . . that guy at the bus
line? . . . ever since I left the . . . you know what I mean?"

"Nope."

Her lips twisted into an almost smile. "You don't talk
much, do you?"

"Nope."

She wriggled slightly until he understood that she wanted
him to turn so she didn't have to keep looking over her shoulder to see where they were going. Too bad. He was getting
kind of used to it.

"See that place up there with the mannequin in the window?"

"The what?"

"The dummy with the suit on."

He nodded.

"We'll get you a coat or something in there, okay? I know
the guy that owns it."

"Fine."

"And some boots for me. My feet are cold."

He nodded.

"Then will you do me a favor?"

Since she had saved him from the howling, vengeful lynch
mob, he reckoned he didn't have much choice. He nodded.

"Will you take me to that Time Thing thing of yours?"

Immediately, every warning flag went up, and he took a
long time before saying, "Why?"

"Because," she said, "I have this awful feeling you're not
as nuts as I think you are."

CHAPTER 2

"Please! Don't shoot!"

Neither Virgil nor Molly had any intention of shooting the creature that had risen out of the depths of the Tennessee River, after first breaking a large hole in the surface. Not only didn't they have anything to shoot it with, they were still too paralyzed with fear to do more than clutch each other and back slowly away as it advanced toward the bank.

It was, in simple terms, something entirely encased in what appeared to be an exotic futuristic metal alloy liberally streaked with grime and wriggling green things that dropped to the ground with every clumsy step it took. Its head resembled a gleaming diver's helmet with a round glass porthole in front and two trembling antennae protruding from the top; its shoulders, torso, and arms resembled those of a burly rain forest gorilla except for the metal alloy that covered them in overlapping plates studded with orange and blue spikes; its legs resembled those of a muscular lowland gorilla wearing metal alloy overlapping plates with sawtooth edges; and its feet didn't look like anything feet ought to look like, including the long spikes where the toes ought to be and weren't, unless they were inside.

It was at least eight feet tall.

Molly and Virgil exchanged fearful, coupled with puzzled, glances.

The creature approached ponderously, stopped at the bottom of the embankment, and looked up at the not quite but close enough cowering humans.

"I am not—"

One of the antennae fell off.

The creature swiveled awkwardly at the waist and peered

down at the river, swiped several times at the fallen equipment, but couldn't lean over far enough to pick it up.

Finally it straightened with a great deal of creaking and clanking, and pointed a metal alloy finger at the two humans, who had backed off as far as they could without spearing themselves on the various protruding sharp parts of the rusted metal contraption abandoned on the riverbank.

"I come in peace!" the creature announced in a pleasantly deep voice.

Large bubbles began to escape into the air from a crack in the porthole through which Virgil was able to see nothing but swirling dark water and what might have been a futuristic goldfish.

"I will not harm you!"

Molly tugged on Virgil's arm, a signal that this thing, whatever it was, clearly wouldn't be quick enough to stop them if they made a break for it. Now.

"Listen to me, Hew Man," the creature said, taking a step onto the bank. "I wish to . . . I am coming in the name of . . . I need to converse with the . . . take me to . . ." The voice faltered, and squealed. "I come in . . . shit, hang on a minute, there's a . . ." It squealed again. "I come in . . . I want to converse with . . ."

It quivered, quaked, and took another clanking step.

"Fear not, for I am come in . . ." Its arms gestured helplessly. "I ask you to take me to . . . I come in . . . goddamnitalltohell!" It battled at the bubbles now flocking around its porthole. "Hew Mans, listen to . . . there is very little time and I must speak with the person in charge of your courageous expedition so that we may coordinate the efforts of our two forces in order to . . . to . . . oh . . . fiddle."

At which point the creature fell flat on its face.

Molly took immediate advantage of the situation by darting out from the dubious protection of the rusted thing and heading for the top of the bank. Virgil, however, after taking a step after her, couldn't help but be fascinated by the floundering beast and the distinctly unbeastlike noises it made while attempting to right itself. Finally his scientific curiosity could stand it no longer, and with a gesture to Molly to hang on a minute, he hurried over, knelt down beside the thing, and frowned as he examined its intricate structure.

"Virge!" Molly whispered loudly. "Come on!"

He shook his head, deepened his frown, and reached for the neck.

"Virgil!"

With a single grunting twist of his powerful hands he detached the helmetlike head, from which dangled after all the water ran out several color-coded wires leading into the body of the beast itself. He smiled and beckoned Molly to come on back. She did, albeit reluctantly, shaking her head until she understood that whatever she thought the thing was, it wasn't.

That's when Virgil pointed to one of the plates in the lower back area.

Molly's eyes widened at the red "Exit" emblazoned thereon.

Virgil rapped a knuckle against it.

The beast kicked its feet so hard they punched a hole in the river.

He rapped it again, shave-and-a-haircut-two-bits.

The metal alloy thing fell still.

"Virgil," Molly said, again in a whisper but quieter than the last one, "it's a machine."

"Looks like it."

"Someone's inside."

"I think so."

"I don't think he can get out."

Virgil grinned. "Yeah. How about that?"

From deep within the caverns of the creature they heard a faint muttering, helpless and pleading.

Virgil, applying all that he had learned from his childhood hero now lost somewhere in the hostile innards of Nashville, considered as many options and consequences as he could in the time given him, which, he also figured, probably wasn't all that long since sooner or later someone would spot a metal gorilla and two green people on the river and the chase would begin all over again.

Then Molly said, "Virgil," and pointed to a puff of smoke that mixed with the weakening bubbles spurting out of the neck where the head used to be.

Virgil wasted no time—he wrenched off the plate, ripped off another, tore off a third, and averting his face from the billows of acrid smoke escaping from the metal alloy body, plunged his hands inside, squinting in intense concentration until at last he grinned, yanked, and fell back with a man firmly in his grasp.

Flames spat from the gorilla's remains.

An ominous rumbling, hissing, and spitting followed soon thereafter.

Virgil didn't need any help from his childhood hero to figure out what was going on—he scrambled to his feet, tucked the semi-conscious man under one arm, and ran for a row of ornamental shrubbery dying at the top of the bank, Molly right beside him. When they reached the shrubs, they bulldozed through, whirled, and dropped to the ground just as the gorilla exploded. Flaming metal, fiery wire, searing assorted nuts and bolts and bits of artificial wood filled the air like demented shrapnel, while a spiral column of fire and black smoke rose toward the sky.

Seconds later the sirens began.

Molly urged Virgil to his feet, her uniform smoking in several interesting places, and together they carried the still semiconscious man across the narrow street and into an alley conveniently located opposite their previous hiding place. It was a dark alley, but not so dark that they couldn't see to the far side and reach it in less time than it took them to estimate the distance to the other side. Once there, they checked both directions before moving quickly to their left, then their right, then into another alley where they made it to the other side without incident.

Across the street was a bar.

Molly patted to extinction her smoking parts and pointed. "We should go in there."

"Good idea," Virgil answered. "It'll be dark, and if the pearls come in, we can sneak out the back."

"That, too," she said. "But I need a drink."

After several vehicles flew noisily past them, oblivious to the turmoil on the river and the fugitives lurking below them, they scurried into the bar and dropped into the first booth they could find, which happened to be by the window. Virgil propped the man up, and checked the place out.

There wasn't much to check—it was dark inside. Almost totally so, except for soft blue neon around the mirror behind the long, polished ebony-and-glass bar, soft blue neon stars here and there on the ceiling, and an only slightly brighter blue neon oval on the back wall, illuminating just enough of the area to show it to be a stage, which, right now, was empty. A score of other booths lined the walls wherever there wasn't the bar or the stage, and from the low murmur of conversation, and the two bartenders, it was clear that they weren't alone, and just as clear that they wouldn't be disturbed; it had that kind of ambiance.

The semi-conscious man moaned softly.

Molly peered at him through the gloom. "Do you think he's hurt?"

"I don't think so, no. Took in some smoke, that's all. He'll live."

"So who is he?"

The man raised his head from the table. "Rowman Barrows," he said, blinked blearily, and suddenly coughed long and hard into a fist Molly noted was rather small. When the painful spasm ebbed, he sat back and rubbed his sooty face with the backs of his hands. "Where am I?"

"A bar," Virgil said, and explained why the metal alloy gorilla machine was still back on the riverbank.

Rowman slapped his forehead with the heel of one hand, slapped his cheek with the palm of the other, and let his head thump back onto the table. He muttered something.

"What?" Molly said.

"He said yow, he's ruined," Virgil answered.

Another mutter, and a frustrated, but light, pounding of the table with both fists.

"What?" Molly said.

"He said everything is royally screwed up, they'll never trust him on the surface again, the entire operation is in jeopardy thanks to him, and now he'll have to emigrate to the Siberian Protectorate where no one will ever find him."

A tiny fist clutched the air dramatically.

The man muttered.

"What?" said Molly.

"He said stop saying what."

"What?"

The man raised his head, sighed, and leaned back, his eyes closed in resigned repose just long enough for Molly to note that he was clearly an older man, perhaps in his early fifties,

with enough hair left to grow partially grey in a distinguished
sort of way, enough lines on his features to indicate someone
who had spent some time in the sun, and a faint scar that ran
a jagged path from the center of his upper lip around the corner of his mouth and down the center of his chin. Where it
went after that she didn't know because the dull silver turtle-
neck shirt with the padded shoulders hid the rest of it. She
also noticed from the size of his arms that he was rather mus-
cularly constructed for a man of his size, which was little.

He coughed again, and punched at his chest.

Virgil slipped out of the booth and went to the bar, spoke
softly with one of the female bartenders, and returned with a
clear plastic tray with three tall, filled, pale blue glasses on it.

"What's that?" Molly asked.

"I ordered the specialty of the house," he said. "Seemed
the safest thing to do."

She sipped. Her eyes watered. Her throat seized. Her chest
fired. "Whiskey," she gasped.

Virgil sipped, licked his lips, and nodded.

Barrows sipped, gagged, sipped, coughed, sipped, sighed,
and leaned back again. "Thanks, stranger," he said.

"No problem."

"I owe you a big one."

"No sweat."

"Whatever you want, just ask."

Molly stared at him over the top of her glass. "What's with
the robot suit?"

Barrows smiled as politely as condescension would permit.
"I wasn't talking to you, lady lady."

"Oops," Virgil said.

"Oops what?" Barrows said just before Molly rose with a
quiet growl, reached over the table, and lifted him up by the
front of his silver shirt, hoisted him easily over to her side,
and plunked him down on his feet beside her.

She didn't release him. However, she did say, in an inex-
cusable fit of two-hundred-year-old political correctness,
"Damn, you're a Little Person."

"Like hell," he snarled proudly. "I'm exactly at the top official height limit for a midget. The only, I might add, lady
lady, midget in the entire GT metropolitan area."

"Throw him back," she said to Virgil.

Barrows paled. "Yow, no! You can't! They'll—"

"Kill you?" she finished.

He fell back against the window, realized what he had done, and dropped to the seat. Nodded weakly. Pulled his glass over and drank deeply. Coughed, gasped, wiped his eyes, and burped loud enough for the bartender to bring them another round.

Virgil hunched his shoulders and leaned forward. "Who're they?"

The strapping midget shook his head.

Molly slid her hand tenderly up his spine until her hand was in perfect position to either massage the back of his head, or snap his neck.

Barrows looked at her sadly. "If I tell you, lady lady, they'll kill you too, no question about it." He gazed forlornly at the table. "You saved my life. I can't repay you by getting you killed."

"No problem," she answered. "I can live with that."

"Absolutely," he told her.

"The underground," Virgil blurted. "Some kind of revolutionaries?"

Molly rolled her eyes, and drank.

Barrows groaned and thunked his head back down onto the table.

"What?" Virgil said.

Barrows mumbled.

Molly sighed. "He said it's not the underground, it's the underriver, they're trying to overthrow the current regime in order to bring participatory democracy back to Greater Tennessee, and you just blew his cover."

"But he wore a metal gorilla suit," Virgil protested. "What kind of cover is that?"

Barrows groaned.

"What?" Virgil said, confusion doing all manner of physically impossible things to his face.

"He said that that big guy in the white suit—the one who was chasing us?—is close to taking over the GT legislature with his cronies and confidants, threatening to ban drugs, music, artificial replacement of limb and ligature, and any car that's bigger than his. He intends to establish a theocracy based on the Hangin' Salvation Gospel Trail and Way of the

Poke, and hang anyone who isn't interested, branded, or out of town by sunset. The metal gorilla suit wasn't his idea. Besides, he was the only one who could fit in it."

"My god," Virgil exclaimed. "We'd better find Diego fast and get the hell out of here before it's too late."

Barrows raised his head. "Diego?"

Virgil nodded.

"You got a friend named Diego?"

Virgil nodded.

The midget looked at Molly. "You got a friend named Diego?"

Molly nodded, even though she didn't want to because she already suspected that acknowledging the connection was going to cause more trouble than the woman in the rattlesnake boots, which were, all in all, pretty damn tacky.

"Yow," Barrows said quietly into his drink. "Yow."

"Meaning?" Molly said irritably.

There was no immediate answer.

There was, however, a growing noise outside, like the approach of a thousand hooves thundering across the tarmac plain. Molly stretched over Barrow's head and tried to locate the source of the noise, looked back and realized no one else in the bar was paying it the slightest attention.

It grew louder.

Barrows slid down in his seat.

"What?" she demanded.

"Buffalo," he said nervously.

She too had learned a few lessons from Virgil's childhood hero—she waited.

"Kind of like the Hangin' Salvation Gospel Auxiliary," he explained. "Bunch of mean and nasty folks who go around beating up on people who aren't yet converted to the truth of the Poke Trail."

"They dress like buffalo," she said.

"Yeah, how did you know?"

She pointed at the Buffalo Herd thundering past the bar, men and women wearing mock buffalo heads, faux buffalo hides cloaked over their shoulders, and phony buffalo feet on their feet. There were nearly a hundred of them, and they raised an impossible amount of dust as they ran by, grunting Buffalo talk and snorting a lot. Someone near the stage tittered nervously, and was hushed loudly by several someone elses. When the Herd finally passed and the dust settled, the silence was loud enough to make Virgil blink.

"Can't the pearls stop them?" he asked.

The midget shook his head. "They try, but they're always outnumbered. Best they do is hover and drive them into streets that don't have too many pedestrians." He shrugged. "Half of them are shinin' anyway, they'd walk off a cliff if Bufoally told them to."

Virgil stared miserably into the night. "Man, I hope Diego is all right."

"Diego?"

"Our friend."

"Nuts."

"What's the matter?"

"I thought y'all were kidding."

"We're not."

"Too bad. If your friend's name really is Diego, or he's just calling himself that—"

"It's his real name," Molly said.

"—then there's no sense hunting for him."

"Why's that?"

" 'Cause that boy's a zombie, you know what I mean?"

"No," Virgil said.

Barrows uttered a short bitter laugh. "Means he's a walking dead man and he don't even know it."

CHAPTER 3

Ferret McJay, looking every bit like his nickname and smelling pretty much like one too, stood back from his customer and nodded his pleasure. "Very elite," he said, his voice high enough to curl cotton. "Just a touch of flash, just

a hint of humble servitude." He nodded again. "You should
have no trouble."

Diego took a superhuman grip on his restraint and said
nothing.

He stood glumly in front of a full-length non-neon mirror
and did his best not to wince, groan, or otherwise exhibit in-
gratitude. He had already seen that fashion in this far-flung
century not his own, and thank the Lord for it encompassed
all manner of style and accessories which, in his own time,
would have gotten most folks shot before they reached the
door. He had hoped, however, that Belle's friend could have
done a little better, considering their mission of trying to return to the TT in more or less one working piece.

Granted the overcoat covered him nicely to the tips of his
boots, and granted it was a reasonably pleasing light grey and
actually fit fairly well across the shoulders, but he wasn't too
sure about the large green rhinestone cactus on the back or the
purple rhinestone wagon wheels over each breast. He had
thought the idea was to render him inconspicuous, and while
he hadn't yet quite grasped the idea of space travel as Belle
had hastily explained it, he was fairly certain the pink rocket
ship–shaped fringe along the sleeves was not going to permit
him to blend into the background.

"Yes, yes," McJay said. "Yes. *Tres* good."

Diego glowered at his reflection.

Belle, huffing on a pair of ordinary tooled-leather boots,
looked up and grinned from under his hat.

"Natural, too," the proprietor declared proudly, stepping
back farther to admire the view. "Never use fakes if I can
help it."

"Natural what?" Diego asked.

"Why . . . cloth, what else?" The man's nose twitched.
"You think I'd pass off a poly or lab cloth on you?"

Wisely Diego kept his mouth shut, such taciturn behavior
having proven invaluable in the Past in keeping others from
knowing that he didn't have a clue what they were talking
about, and probably wouldn't have understood it even if he
did. Grunting and nodding usually did the job just fine.

He grunted and nodded.

Meanwhile, Belle stood, stamped around the cluttered floor
to test her new boots and get her toes the rest of the way in,

and suggested to the dark-suited ferret that he really ought to
start stocking footwear in matched pairs; boots of different
sizes tended to anger the feet and made people walk funny.
The man shrugged unconcernedly, reminding her that his was
a business that catered to the lost, the desperate, and the fugitive from justice types, who didn't exactly have a whole lot
of choice, even if they did walk funny. She reminded him that
he was a fugitive himself and ought to have a little more sym-
pathy. He reminded her that she owed him money. She reminded him that her initial request had been coupled with the
information that she didn't have a cent on her and would have
to owe him. He reminded her that his was a cash-and-carry
business, and if payment wasn't forthcoming soon, he knew a
few good fellows who could use a night's work. She told him
to go to hell and close the door behind him. He told her she
was the only hooker he'd ever met who didn't hook, but
maybe they could work something out.

Diego, who intended to yank the rocket ship fringe off the
moment he left the shop, stepped into the middle of the conversation by opening his godawful new topcoat and reminding the ferret what those things were he had strapped around
his waist.

McJay's nose twitched again, and he allowed as how he
and Belle had been friends for a long time, he trusted her, and
she shouldn't feel pressured getting back to him with the balance of her debt. Then, smiling toothily, he reached into his
gold lamé vest and pulled out a rectangular box with an obscene cameo set in its lid. He thumbed it open and offered the
contents.

"To show no hard feelings," he said graciously.

Diego saw several tiny compartments inside, in which were
even tinier or they wouldn't have fit otherwise capsules of
varying colors. He looked at Belle, who said contemptuously,
"Shine."

"Like that fella outside before?"

She nodded. "It goes straight to the nerve endings, sparks
'em all to hell, makes you think you're invincible, intelligent,
and able to see in the dark."

"Perfect description," said the ferret, snapping the pill box
closed.

"It also makes you stupid," she added. "And your eyes

glow. Sooner or later they don't stop glowing, and you go
blind, deaf, and your fingers fall off."

"Rumor," McJay scoffed. "Never saw anybody without any
fingers."

"So why does anyone use it?" Diego asked, recalling a
couple of half-breed peyote-chompers he had met in Arizona
who thought they could fly after meeting the spirits one night
at the edge of the Grand Canyon. The fact that they could indeed fly didn't surprise him; the fact that they couldn't
change direction did. Didn't make much sense to him if flying
downward was about the only thing the spirits could do for
you. But then, he supposed spirits were like that, which was
why they were spirits and he was stuck in a shop with a man
that smelled like a wet cow.

Belle only snorted and marched toward the door.

McJay leaned as close to Diego as he could without Diego
passing out and whispered, "Makes you sexier'n hell, that's
why. I heard one guy lasted all week."

Okay, Diego thought; that's a fair reason to be stupid.

"Nice funeral, too," McJay added regretfully. "Seemed like
half the females in GT were there." He sighed, shook himself
to banish the melancholy memory, and dusted idly at Diego's
shoulders. "If you need any alterations, or if the 'stones start
falling off, you come on back, you hear? No charge for the
fixing."

"I'll remember that."

"You'll be too dead if you don't stop jawing," Belle called
from the doorway. "Can we get it moving here?"

Diego would have answered had not a distant rumbling
caught his attention and made him listen whether he wanted
to or not; oddly enough, it almost sounded familiar. Behind
him, McJay whimpered; in front of him, Belle ducked back
into the shop and said, "The Herd."

"Beeswax," the ferret cursed. "I was going to eat out tonight too."

A quick explanation made Diego's fingers itch.

"They won't come into the Alley," McJay assured them
tentatively. "Right, Belle?"

She shrugged ambiguously. "Never have before." A long
look at Diego. "But if they're stampeding for what I think
they're stampeding for, I wouldn't bet on it, either."

The thunder grew.

Feathers and plumes trembled.

McJay vanished behind a stack of freestanding rhinestones.

Diego and Belle backed away from the door, Diego searching through the gloom for a rear exit, a window, or a trapdoor just in case a retreat would be wiser than getting himself trampled, which, when he thought about it further, made him look even harder.

The thunder grew.

The feathers and plumes vibrated.

McJay poked his head above the rhinestones, whimpered, and vanished again.

And just as Diego thought the Herd would indeed come into the Alley and destroy or dent everything and everyone in its path, the thunder began to fade.

"We can't wait any longer," Belle told him, settled his hat firmly on her head, and rushed outside, swinging left and stopping as if she had hit a wall before Diego had even reached the threshold.

"Hell," she muttered in disgust.

There, not ten feet away, was a white Indian and a cowgirl, who looked depressingly familiar when Diego glanced around the jamb.

"Well, well, well," the cowgirl said, tenderly caressing the curved hilts of her matched machetes. "Looks like we got a sinner here, Roy."

The white Indian grinned widely and took a yellowhead tomahawk from the sagging belt that just barely held up his loincloth. "You know, Sara," he said, "maybe we can kinda convert her, you know what I mean?"

The cowgirl chuckled.

Belle couldn't move; her new boots had gotten stuck in a puddle of semi-liquid.

"You bait and hook, girly girl, hook and bait?" the cowgirl asked snidely. "You lookin' to end your miserable career early tonight?"

"Maybe," Diego said, calmly stepping out of the shop. "Maybe not."

"Oooh, Sara," the white Indian said in mock terror. "Oooh, mercy, I'm *so* afraid."

"Mister," the cowgirl said, "you got twenty-four hours to get out of my town."

Diego's right hand eased back for his gun, found a rocket ship instead, and froze, slightly confused by an apparent appearance of a technology it wasn't used to.

Desperately, Belle grabbed her shin and tried to free her right foot.

The white Indian shook his head and tsked. "You ain't much good at hooking, are you, girly girl?"

He laughed heartily, and the cowgirl joined him.

"Not funny," Diego said.

The white Indian spat against the wall. "Ain't talking to you, mister."

"Twenty-four hours," the cowgirl reminded him.

Diego reached for his left-hand gun, found another rocket ship, and growled, tore off the godawful coat, grabbed his hat from Belle's head, and put it on.

Then he brushed back his jacket.

"Seems you already told me that once," he said to the cowgirl.

The white Indian paled and staggered back a step.

The cowgirl clearly couldn't believe her eyes. She wiped them several times, stared, and swallowed hard and loudly. Twice she attempted to reach for her machetes, and twice she changed her mind and wiped her eyes again.

"Diego," Belle cautioned.

"What?" the white Indian yelled.

"What?" the cowgirl shouted.

Diego flexed his fingers.

The cowgirl whooped, shoved the white Indian aside, and pelted back up the Alley as fast as her feet and the semi-liquid would permit.

The white Indian, however, stood his ground.

Belle did too, but not for the same reason.

"Move along," Diego suggested mildly. "No need for a fuss."

The white Indian, ignoring Sara's cries to get his white Indian ass out of there, merely tapped the tomahawk against his leg, winced, and turned it around, tapped it again. "Blasphemer," he snarled.

Diego said nothing.

"Defiler of the Trail," the white Indian growled.

Diego said nothing.

McJay whimpered from behind his stack of by now unstable rhinestones.

The white Indian's eyes narrowed when his threats seemed to have no effect. After due consideration, his shoulders squared, his legs stiffened, and slowly, very slowly, he raised the tomahawk over his head.

"Don't," Diego warned.

Belle tried freeing the other foot and lost her balance, fell against the wall and slid to the ground. When she swore, the puddle shimmered and her boot popped out.

"Hangin's too good for you," the white Indian said.

Diego sighed.

"Blasphemer!"

"You said that already," Diego told him wearily.

"Did not."

"Yep."

"Didn't!"

"Not two minutes ago."

The white Indian looked to Belle. "Did I already say that?"

Belle nodded.

The white Indian frowned, looked up at his weapon gleaming lethally in the dim light, and said, "Nuts."

He threw the tomahawk.

Diego drew.

Belle cried out.

Diego fired.

Twice.

The first bullet neatly split the tomahawk's haft, sending the two pieces harmlessly against the Alley wall, except for the bottom part that clunked off Belle's head and knocked her back into the wall, and the top half that spun into the shop where McJay yelped instead of whimpered when all the rhinestones fell and buried him.

The second bullet punched the white Indian off his feet and into a puddle, which bubbled enthusiastically.

"Up," Diego ordered, looked down when nothing happened, and saw Belle, dazed, rubbing her head. He grabbed her hand, yanked her to her feet, and held on until he was sure she could stand on her own. Then he hustled up the Alley, past the bubbling dead guy, scowled, and hustled back, shaking his head as Belle tried and failed to pop the other boot out of its obscenely clinging puddle.

"Your foot," he said impatiently.

"What?"

"Take your damn foot out of the boot and let's get out of here."

"Jesus," she muttered. But she did as she was told and hustle-limped with him, slowing only when she had to hop another puddle, except when she passed what was still left of the white Indian.

She looked down. "Jesus."

Diego kept moving.

"Right between the eyes."

Faces appeared in windows and doorways, and disappeared just as quickly when they saw who they were looking at and didn't believe that who they were looking at dared look like that, not in this day and age. Clothes like that more or less got you hanged.

He heard Belle hop-limp-running to catch up, felt her take his arm, looked down and saw the expression on her face. This, he thought, is getting wearisome.

"Later," he said.

She didn't argue.

At the Alley's mouth they checked the street for signs that weren't practically shouting, yelling, flickering, buzzing neon, and only saw a large cloud of dust moving away from them to the north. Plus a battered Buffalo lying in the gutter, his horns bent all to hell, his hide virtually stripped from his back. He groaned and tried to sit up as they hurried by, fell back again and flopped his legs onto the pavement. Diego saw that the bruised and bloodied young man wore curious small round metal balls on his feet.

"Keep that in mind," Belle said. "A lesson from the Trail of the Poke."

Diego wondered, but didn't ask, figuring she was going to tell him anyway, even if he didn't want to know, which he didn't, and she did:

"You can't rollerskate in a Buffalo Herd."

"Thanks."

"Don't mention it."

"What's a rollerskate?"

"Better to ask what's that?"

"What's what?"

She pointed.

He didn't ask.

About three blocks away and twenty stories up, and descending fast, was a long white car with longhorn horns bolted to its nose, the choir singing, the trumpet blaring, and a brawny man in a white suit standing on the hood, holding on to a pair of reins tied to the horns.

He pointed down and cried, "Blasphemer! Repent! Your day has come!"

And someone on the street cried, "Hot damn, Horace, there's gonna be a hangin'!"

CHAPTER 4

"We've got to get back to the TT," Molly insisted heatedly. "Sitting here isn't getting us anywhere."

"What's a TT?" Barrows asked.

"No time to explain. You have any money, or whatever it is you use here?"

The midget nodded.

She nodded sharply. "Good. Pay the bartender for this stuff, we'll owe you."

Barrows drew himself up indignantly. "Now wait a minute, Miss Molly. You can't go ordering me around when I was kindly enough to—"

"We saved your life," Virgil reminded him. "And we haven't got time to argue. Every minute we waste is another minute less Diego has someone to watch his back."

"Suppose I don't want to leave?"

Molly shrugged angrily as she stood. "Stay. Leave. Come with us. I don't care. Virgil, let's go."

They hurried out of the bar, turned left, ran a dozen paces, looked puzzledly at each other, changed their minds and went the other way. Twenty steps later, they muttered, changed their minds again and headed back in the other direction. Each time they passed the bar, Barrows waved politely from the booth and toasted their good fortune, health, and long life; each time they changed their minds, Molly growled about being dumb enough to get lost in a damn barn, for god's sake, and Virgil complained that if she knew so damn much, why the hell didn't she find someone to ask directions from.

Finally, after the midget mimed offering her a drink the fifth or sixth time she saw him, she threw up her hands in defeat, ducked back into the bar, emptied Barrows' glass herself, and yanked him from his seat.

"Hey!"

"You pay?"

"Of course. I know how to—"

She carried him outside, plunked him down on the pavement, gestured angrily up and down the empty street, and said, "Which way is the railroad station, and don't give me any of your crap about oppressive governments, reinstated democracies, or bloodthirsty hangin' preachers or I'll shove you back in what's left of your gorilla suit."

Barrows looked from one to the other. "Y'all are really serious about getting your friend, ain't you?"

She scowled.

"Rowman, look at it this way," Virgil said. "You helping us will make Bufoally look like an idiot. Not many preachers, even in our own Time, held on to their congregations when they ended up looking like idiots. Think of it as a way to serve the Cause and stop that demagogue from taking over and ruining the city state, and the country, you love."

"What Cause?"

Molly reached for his throat.

Virgil grabbed her wrist in a practiced restraining hold and said, "The Revolutionary Cause."

"Oh." Barrows kicked glumly at the sidewalk. "Some Cause. They made me wear a gorilla suit."

"Okay, okay," Molly said impatiently, shaking her wrist free. "Forget the Cause. What about making Bufoally look like an idiot?"

"Dangerous man, Miss Molly," he said. "You cross him, and he'll try to hang you for sure. And you can be golly damn sure the pearls aren't going to help, not with you being strangers and wearing green underwear and all."

"I don't want to cross him, for god's sake," she snapped, her face reddening dangerously. "I just want to make him look like an idiot!"

"Well, that's okay then." He clapped his hands, rubbed his palms together with burning enthusiasm, and said, "So where are we going?"

"The railroad station."

"What railroad station?"

CHAPTER 5

They hadn't run through two featureless alleys before Diego made Belle take off her other boot. He claimed it was making him dizzy, watching her bob up and down like that. She snapped that it wasn't her fault, those puddles are what's left of shiners when they've lost their shine, and she'd be damned and double-damned if she'd be held responsible for some fool drug addict trying to steal her boots, even in his semi-liquid state. He snapped back that Bufoally's chariot was fast coming around the far corner, and if she wanted to fight, could she please wait until they got where they were going.

"Where are we going?"

"The railroad station."

"The what?"

"The railroad station. Maybe my friends have gone back there, looking for me."

"You mean . . ." She waved both hands in a vague approximation of a direction. ". . . where all this started? Where I met you?"

"Yep."

She stopped. "Nope."

He stopped, turned, and used his best, most intimidating *I hope I didn't hear what I thought I just heard* voice. "What do you mean, nope?"

The celestial trumpet sounded the resumption of the chase as the white chariot that looked pretty much like a car with humongous tail fins hove into view sweeping not five feet above the street.

"That's where they hang people like you, remember?"

The distinct thunder of the Buffalo Herd rose from the cross street opposite them.

"Well, that's where the damn train is," he said.

"Blasphemer!" bellowed Bufoally from his standing position on the chariot's hood.

Diego cursed and ran, ducking into yet another alley, this one barely wide enough for his shoulders. He heard Belle's feet slapping the ground behind him, and he wondered why in hell she stuck around when she knew damn well that sticking around, in the non-puddle sense, would very likely get her killed. Not that he minded her sticking around, he thought as he vaulted a crushed crate; it was kind of nice having someone around when you're pretty sure you're going to die. Of course, the last time it happened to him, it wasn't a person but a coyote who kept trying to eat his hat; but at least it was company.

And breakfast, which is how he had gotten out of that particular scrape alive.

A glance over his shoulder and over Belle's no longer bobbing head showed him a blur of white zooming past the alley mouth, no doubt intent on cutting him off at the pass, wherever that was. However, he reckoned that if he kept heading uphill, sooner or later he'd be close to that spot where the first riot began, and from there he would be able to make his way into the station and thus, with some incredible luck and a stroke of magnificent stupidity on the part of his pursuers, to safety.

The Buffalo Herd exploded one at a time into the alley.

The preacher's chariot air-skidded around the corner, squealed, and took off a chunk of a disappointingly ordinary brick building, nearly throwing Bufoally from his figurative but still slippery saddle.

Diego whirled to his left and ran harder, ignoring a growing stitching in his injured side as he cut diagonally across the street and around the next corner. He knew he wouldn't be able to outrun that chariot thing, but if it kept knocking into buildings the way it was, maybe it'd slow down long enough for him to find someplace to hide until it went past.

Belle caught up.

The white chariot air-skidded around the corner behind them and crumpled its tail fins against a glass wall.

The preacher yelled.

The Buffalo Herd began to emerge one at a time from the alley and reform its thundering pursuit.

Belle tripped.

CHAPTER 6

"A drainpipe?" Molly squawked in disbelief. "This is some kind of future joke, right? A . . . drainpipe?"

Barrows studied the small metal-rimmed hole bored into the side of the high curb, looked at Molly, looked at Virgil, and sighed. "Habit, Miss Molly, sorry. They always made me go down there, so I could come up somewhere else and do some spying on whoever was oppressing us at the time."

"Seems to me they took advantage of you," Virgil said.

"Tell me about it," he muttered.

"Well, let's see . . . first there was that dumb gorilla suit, and then—"

Molly stamped her foot to shut him up, then spun around when she heard the distant cry of a heavenly choir, a blatting trumpet, and the Buffalo Herd. "We gotta motor, boys!"

Barrows frowned.

"Move!" she said.

"Where?"

"The train station!"

"Great! Follow me!"

He started to run, stopped, and looked back. "Well?"

Molly did her best not to strangle Virgil since he was closer than Barrows and couldn't run as fast. "You said you didn't know where the train station was."

"I thought you said the rain station. Hell, everybody knows where the train station is."

"Why?" Virgil asked. "Do they still use trains?"

"Nope. They just hang people there."

Molly ran, Barrows ran, and Virgil ran until he passed Molly and Barrows, slowed up until Molly caught up with him, and ran again until they both had to slow down until Barrows caught up with them, and the three of them ran to the next corner, turned it, and ran on, Virgil waiting until Molly caught up, then the two of them waiting until Barrows caught up, then running on until Virgil stopped, waited until Barrows caught up a third time, and lifted him unapologetically onto his shoulder.

"Don't mean to be offensive," he panted as he started to run again, after making sure Molly wasn't left behind.

"No sweat," Barrows assured him as he clung to the tall hefty bald young man's head. "My feet were killing me anyway. Golly, you have no idea how cramped that gorilla suit was, especially when you have company. Next time I want a chipmunk or I ain't going." He patted Virgil's pate. "You just run, big fella, I'll tell you where."

"Right," Virgil said.

"No! Left!"

"Don't start that," Molly warned them. "Do. Not. Start. Just . . . do it."

"Right," Virgil said.

"No!" Barrows cried, almost too late. "Left!"

"A gun," Molly muttered hysterically. "Where the hell is a gun? Why isn't there ever a gun around when—"

With a snap of her fingers she remembered the butter knife tucked in her breast pocket, but by then the two men had charged around another corner. She sighed, picked up speed, and took the corner too fast to avoid colliding with Virgil's back, which had stopped with the rest of him when he saw the Buffalo Herd sprinting and thundering left to right across

the far intersection, just ahead of a long white and very
dented chariot car with longhorn horns bolted to its nose.

A man stood on the hood, holding a pair of ragged reins,
and shouting, "Blasphemer! Hang the blasphemer!"

A choir sang.

A trumpet sounded.

"Damn," she said. "Diego."

She ran.

Virgil and Barrows caught up half a block later, the midget
having shifted so that he straddled Virgil's neck and held on
by gripping the tall man's forehead.

Then Barrows said, "What did you mean when you said,
even in our time?"

"Later," she gasped.

"Right," Virgil gasped.

"No!" Barrows yelled, just as a fleet of pearls flew into the
street behind them.

CHAPTER 7

"I'm sorry," Belle said breathlessly as Diego scooped her
up and ran on.

"There was nothing there," he complained.

"I said I was sorry. It was just something I felt I had to do.
Kind of like instinct, I guess."

"Do you feel like running?"

She looked over his shoulder. "Yes."

He put her down. "Then run!"

She did.

He did too, until he realized the utter futility and complete
foolishness of trying to outrun a flying car that was supposed
to be a chariot, and a bunch of fanatics dressed like buffalo
after a bad winter. Besides, although continuing to move uphill was still a good idea, the uphill part was killing his legs,

his lungs, and various other numbed parts of him. So when the trumpet signaled another turn, he swerved sharply to his right, grabbing Belle's elbow along the way, and plunged into a shop whose display window, he noted as he banged in the door, was about as tasteful as any he had seen since he'd arrived; tasteful, of course, being a matter of taste.

Once inside, they wove frantically around several free-standing shelves holding gaudy ornamental items obviously intended for those Nashvillian patrons who had more money than sense, and ran toward a sales counter at the back. At which stood, Diego saw with not much amazement because that's the way things were going, a skinny ferret in a snug black suit and gold lamé vest dusting a diamond-shaped crystal in which was encased a polished nugget of river sludge.

"My god!" Ferret McJay gasped.

Diego and Belle dove behind the counter just as the chariot whooshed by.

"What are you doing in here?" McJay demanded nervously.

The Buffalo Herd thundered past.

"You can't stay here!" McJay protested.

Diego unholstered his gun. "How often you reckon I miss at this range?"

McJay nearly dropped the crystal in his haste to nod, move away, and try to appear casual when a Buffalo straggler slammed open the door.

"You see anybody?" the man demanded.

McJay shook his head vigorously.

The man lifted his buffalo head so he could see better. "Nice stuff you got in here."

"Thank you."

"That there glass boot on the wall—it lunar?"

McJay eased away from the counter. "Why, yes. Would you like me to—"

The man settled his head back on. "Nah. Gotta hang some guy tonight."

"Too bad."

"Yeah, but you know how it is." The man turned to leave, and changed his mind. "Hey. You a Poke?"

"I beg your pardon."

The Buffalo grunted his righteous disgust. "Heathen."

"I do my best," McJay said stiffly, and gently eased the man outside. "Do come again. There's a sale next week."

The Buffalo grunted, snorted, and shot out of the doorway when the trumpet sounded the charge several blocks away. McJay hastily switched off the tastefully awful neon in the window, pulled down the segmented steel-plate shades, and slumped against the door.

"You can come out now."

Diego stood, gun still in hand. "Obliged," he said as Belle rose beside him.

"Damn right," McJay said.

"Ferret," Belle said, "what in blue-sky blazes are you doing here?"

"It's my day job, if you must know," he answered huffily.

"It's near midnight."

McJay sighed. Loudly. Ran his skinny fingers through his short hair, pinched his twitching nose, and sighed again. Loudly. "All right," he said at last. "I suppose you have a right to know."

"Nope," she said, sitting on the counter. "You got two places, two incomes, both are steals, what the hell." She arranged her sharp sleeve pleats more to her liking. "Don't suppose you have any boots, huh?"

"Please," he said, insulted. "Remember where you are."

Diego remembered, and in doing so came out from behind the counter, holstered his gun, and said, "Time's short, Belle. I figure a couple of blocks, no more." He headed for the door. "You stay here, it's safer."

"With him?" she said, jumping to the floor. "He's got more hands than a whatever has more hands than a person does."

McJay, who apparently had taken a liking to the way he sounded when he sighed, sighed. "They'll get you if you go out there, you know."

"Don't think so. I don't have far."

McJay touched his arm. "Believe me, mister. They'll get you."

"How do you know that?"

The man looked apologetically at Belle, then pointed at Diego's silver-threaded vest. "I slipped a shine cap into your vest back in the Alley." Another sigh, this one artfully, if somewhat melodramatically, laced through with guilt. "It's a homing device."

Diego waited.

Belle said, "It's a way of tracking you electronically, Diego, and can I have one of your guns, I want to shoot the sonofabitch."

"You can shoot?" Diego asked as McJay whimpered, cowered, and pushed himself into the corner.

"What's to know? You aim, you pull the trigger. Just like a laze pistol, except it's louder, has a kick, and is messier than all hell." She picked up a large geode from a shelf. "Never mind. I'll brain him instead."

McJay whimpered.

Diego fingered the capsule from his pocket, held it close to his eye, and couldn't figure out how this tiny thing could let other people know where he was, and where he had been. But if the ferret was telling the truth . . .

"No," Belle said not very convincingly.

Diego drew.

"Oh my," she said.

Diego aimed at the ferret's mouth. "Open wide."

McJay shook his head.

Diego cocked the hammer.

McJay let a tear slip from his left eye, the right one being too busy fighting off a violent tic.

Diego stretched out his arm so that the muzzle was less than six inches from the ferret's pointy nose. "You reckon to bleed a lot?"

"I hate blood."

Diego took a deep breath, the better to steady his aim.

McJay pleaded with Belle not to let this madman do this heinous thing. Belle replaced the geode and suggested that McJay either take his chance with the pill, and the Buffalo Herd, or hope that Diego's hand shakes when he pulls the trigger, thus doing no more damage than ripping off an ear and putting a hole in the wall. McJay flattened himself against the wall as best he could considering all the shelves on it, lifted his chin, and opened his mouth. Belle winced and held her breath.

Diego snatched a petite genuine artificial tiger's eye replica marble from a subdued display behind him and popped it into the man's mouth. "Swallow," he ordered.

After hesitating just long enough to feel the cold steel of the Special brush across his lips, McJay swallowed, sagged groaning to the floor, and rocked side to side while he whimpered.

Diego told Belle to open the steel plates so they could open the door. When she did, one hand clamped over her mouth to stifle the laughter, he checked the street, braced himself, and ran. Belle followed, not asking why Diego had kept the homing capsule, and not having to when he reached the far side and flicked it through a sewer grate, then veered uphill again and found himself on the same street where Belle had first showed him the Special locket around her neck.

Slowly, but not so slowly that his legs cramped, he moved up the right side, keeping as close as he could to the shops and office entrances without actually going inside although he was tempted a couple of times. At the same time he listened hard for the whoosh of the chariot, the thunder of the Herd, the cries of the pursuit, the high notes of the choir, the betrayal of the trumpet; and though he heard nothing but his and Belle's labored breathing, he wasn't relieved. It had occurred to him that the chariot could be hovering hundreds of feet above him and he wouldn't know it, even if he looked up, because it would be too small to distinguish from the other flying automobiles that constantly ghosted through the city; besides, his hat would fall off.

At the top of the slope he pressed against the corner building and peered quickly around the corner.

"Empty," he whispered.

"It could be a trap," she said.

"Guess I'll have to take that chance."

At that moment, with those brave words, the lights went out.

CHAPTER 8

"Damn, I can't see!"

"Hush, Virgil, all the lights went out."

"How can you tell? I can't see a thing."

"Rowman, where do we go from here?"

"Well, Miss Molly, it's only a couple blocks down the hill there."

"What hill? I can't see!"

"Hush, Virgil! Rowman, isn't there any other way?"

"Not aboveground, no."

"Nuts."

"Rowman, get your finger out of my eye!"

"Sorry. It's dark."

"Will you two please be quiet?"

"Sorry."

"Sorry. But damnit, Moll, he had his finger in my eye."

"Look—"

"How?"

"I have a knife and I know how to use it."

"She does?"

"It's a butter knife, Rowman, don't worry, she won't use it."

"What's a butter knife?"

"I'm leaving."

"What's butter?"

"Virge, are you coming or what?"

"Virgil. And I'm right behind you."

"I'm getting airsick."

"There! Look there, Virgil. That glow? It's the station, I'm sure of it. Those floodlights must be on batteries or something."

"Okay, yeah, I see it. So do we run or not?"

"I vote for running."

"Me, too."

"I'm airsick, I tell you."

"One. Two. Three. Go!"

"Diego, look over there."

"Damn, it's them."

"Still have that green underwear, too."

"They're heading for the station."

"So why are we still standing here?"

"There's three of them. See?"

"What? Oh. Lord, don't worry, it's only one of those Free Greater Tennessee and Clean The River Revolutionaries. You can tell by the dopey silver uniforms they wear. What are you afraid of?"

"He may be armed. He may be holding them hostage."

"He's a midget, Diego."

"Still—"

"Besides, he's throwing up."

"Jesus."

"My feet are getting cold, can we go now?"

"My god, Virge, it's Diego!"

"By god, Belle, we're gonna make it."

in the distance, floating through the fairy spires and musical instrument and sheet music and ordinary non-contemporary oddly-out-of-place buildings of abruptly somnolent Nashville, comes the plaintive sound of a trumpet summoning its charging charges back from a charge that had lost its target and most of its oomph;

and even farther in the distance, weaving through the dark night except for the winking red lights at the tops of all the amazing buildings in Nashville, comes the mournful wail of a frustrated pearl whose bullet car hurls from shadow to shadow as it whirls through the night and performs steep curls through side street and alley before it furls its wheel wings and slinks back to its post near the banks of the river, Burma Shave, but not many people do;

and across the darkened street from Union Station, a ferret-face man in a snug black suit and gold lamé vest watches five fugitives race up the steps and into the depths of the deserted greystone structure, nods to himself, and slinks off to the south, toward the largest indoor-outdoor jungle in the world, to meet with his master and collect his reward so he can return to his shop and pick up all the marbles.

And in the station itself, Diego stopped Belle with a touch to her arm.

"You see him?" he said quietly, while the others raced on.

She nodded.

"Didn't scare him enough, I guess."

"What are we going to do?"

He rubbed his chin thoughtfully, then holstered his gun. "Go home, I reckon. He won't be back before I leave."

He walked on quickly, long strides taking him to the head of the inner staircase just as Virgil slammed through the door below. He turned to say something to Belle then, and realized she wasn't there.

She stood in the center of the deserted great hall, a single shaft of the light cutting through the black above her hair.

You don't know her, he told himself.

She didn't move.

She's a woman of the streets, for god's sake, even if she didn't do anything.

She stood there. Alone.

By the time you're in her Past, which will be your Present and Virgil's and Molly's Past, she'll have forgotten all about you; you'll be nothing more than a bad dream about losing two pair of boots.

She pulled her long ponytail over her shoulder.

Damn, he thought.

He held out his hand.

She hesitated.

He waited.

She began to run.

He waited.

She began to hop and skip side to side, yipping and hissing and waving her arms in the air.

He waited.

She finally stopped and said, "Damnit, Diego, now I got splinters. You going to carry me or what?"

And Molly whispered from the bottom of the stairs, "All aboard, cowboy. It's time to go home."

PART IV

Bunkhouse Blues

CHAPTER 1

Every once in a while Diego liked to get himself up on a horse that wasn't aiming to break speed records between North Platte and Denver, and just ride out into the desert or onto the prairie, and wander a little. He did his best to stay away from trains, trails, and the occasional pissed-off Indian looking to take something back to his sweetheart besides a prairie chicken for the evening's stew pot; he also tried to avoid thinking about past jobs, possible future jobs, and the way the horse seemed to wake up every damn rattlesnake in the county; thirdly, he made sure he'd brought along enough food for when he got lost, which was pretty much every time he stayed away from trains and trails, because there wasn't anything worse than having to grub the land for roots, berries, and that prairie chicken whose culinary reputation was considerably blown out of proportion. So was the prairie dog's, for that matter. Snippy damn things, too.

And while he rode, he savored the isolation, the tranquility, the comforting immutability of the immense sky, the sweep and climb of the land, the gold sun and the diamond stars, the sounds that no city dude would ever hear because he was making too much noise building a house that would, sure as God made mothers and little children, collapse in the next strong wind.

He contemplated.

He evaluated.

He renewed himself and his purpose in life.

Then he would ride like hell to the nearest town because a man could take only so much serenity and solitude before he started casting funny looks at his horse and thinking that roots and grubs actually did taste like chicken.

All this, and more, passed through his mind as he stood by the TT's engine, comforted by its sleek boiler, and by the solid feel of the red-rimmed wheels.

He was outside because inside, while Virgil worked at slipping the timer chip into place, Molly worked at trying to explain to Rowman exactly how Time Travel was possible. But the harder she worked, the more questions he asked, most of them having to do with the possibility of going back in Time before the idiot who invented the metal alloy gorilla was born so he could make sure the idiot wasn't born and maybe he'd get something else to wear. He wasn't too thrilled about the silver outfit, either, could she do something about that, too?

On the other hand, Belle had done little more than listen as politely as she could for several minutes before giving Diego a curious, almost melancholy, look, announce that it was too late to be jawing, and curled up on one of the beds, her face to the wall.

Diego, sans hat and jacket, left shortly after that.

After he had taken the butter knife from Molly.

Now he looked up at the dripping ceiling, looked at the pitiful corpses of the other trains, and couldn't help that feeling again—that he was in a graveyard.

He thought about all he had seen outside, and all he had seen back in New York City; he thought about Belle hopping around like water on a hot skillet; he thought about vehicles that flew, vehicles that flew sideways, shops that openly sold women and drugs and marbles and coats with rocket-ship fringe; he thought about maybe thinking too much would give him a headache, but he couldn't stop it.

Something was wrong here.

He thought about the dead white Indian in a puddle that used to be a man.

He thought about the man they called a mule kneeling in the street so that the Reverend Hiram Bufoally could stand on his back and preach the Hangin' Salvation Gospel to a crowd ready to riot.

He thought about Belle's pleated sleeves and how, with just a little effort, she could slice a man to ribbons just by slapping his face.

Something was definitely wrong here.

A quiet footstep turned him around.

Barrows stood near the platform, scratching his head. "You know," the little man said, "I truly do believe y'all came from the Past, really I do. I just can't get it through my head that it's possible."

"I'm here," Diego said simply.

Barrows stared, then shrugged. "Yep. I do guess you are." He shrugged again. "Ain't that a bitch, huh?" And he climbed back inside.

Diego was about to turn around again when Belle leaned over the platform railing. "Bare feet," she said, pointing to the gravel in explanation of why she didn't come down.

He walked toward her slowly.

"Noisy in there," she said.

He nodded.

A wan smile as she pulled her ponytail over her shoulder, making him wonder why she didn't just nail it there, she used it so much.

When he stood beneath her, he could see the age in her face for the first time, the tiny lines about her eyes, the years in her expression. No, he thought; not a girl at all.

"I've been up front, talking to Virgil," she said. "He told me about that Book he read when he was a kid."

Wrong, Diego thought; and getting worse.

"I think it's the same Book Bufoally uses."

He said nothing.

She leaned over farther and looked up the length of the train. "What do you think?"

He followed her gaze. "Tell you the truth, I think folks that put needles on their skin to listen to music, that put false dreams in their veins to listen to their minds, that put steer horns on things that fly . . ." He sighed.

She waited.

"I want to go home, Belle. Damn, I want to go home."

Her hand brushed lightly over his hair, lingered for a moment before pulling away.

He didn't look at her.

"It ain't you, and it ain't them two in there. It's pretty simple actually—I don't belong here. I didn't belong back in that New York City. You don't have to tell me, but I bet there isn't a mile of clear land anywhere anymore. I bet they have houses on the Rockies, and them flying things cutting all over Old Mexico. I bet most of the rivers are like this one you got here." He sniffed, and rubbed the back of his neck. "I bet, even if I'm wrong about that other stuff, that there ain't a place for a man to ride." A quick laugh. "Assuming they still got horses, that is."

"Hey," she whispered.

He did look at her then.

"I don't know you but a short time, Belle, and if anything would get me to stick around, see what's going on, it'd be you." He gave her a smile that made her look away. "But I just don't belong here. A man like me ... I wouldn't know what to do in a place like this. I'd be ..."

He stared at the ground.

"Out of your Time," she said.

He nodded.

"Molly and Virgil," she went on, "I'll bet their Time is closer to mine than it is to yours, in a manner of speaking."

"Yep. And truer than you know."

She touched his hair again, and when he looked up, she kissed him. A slow, sweet kiss sad enough to make the Devil weep.

When she pulled away, there were tears in her eyes, and when she spoke, she spoke hoarsely:

"Damn, but you really are him, aren't you?"

He didn't move for a time longer than seemed possible in the short time it took for him to finally nod.

Then he waited for it, but this time he didn't mind.

CHAPTER 2

"You really are the man they call ... Diego."

CHAPTER 3

And when the sound returned, except for the harmonica interlude which he really missed and wished someone had thought to bring one along, he straightened, grabbed the railing and hauled himself easily up to the platform, grabbed Belle around the waist, hauled her close, kissed her not at all sadly, and opened the door just in time to see Virgil come through the hatch, clap his hands, and say:

"All right! We're ready to rock 'n' roll!"

Molly and Rowman stopped arguing.

Belle squeezed past Diego and threw herself onto one of the loveseats.

Diego wanted to ask what rock 'n' roll was, but he didn't trust himself to find the right words.

"Going home, partner," Virgil told him with a satisfied grin. "Won't be long now before you're back in the saddle again."

Rowman applauded. "Yeah! Out where a friend is a friend that doesn't make you a gorilla suit."

Molly laughed. "And where, I suppose, the longhorn cattle feed or whatever they do on the lonely jimsonweed, whatever the hell that is but I bet you can't cook it worth a damn, right?"

Virgil chuckled.

"I still can't go, huh?" Rowman asked then.

"Sorry," Molly told him. "If you did—"

"Mess up Time and all that, I suppose."

She frowned. "What? Don't be silly, no. What I was going to say—"

"It's because I'm a midget, isn't it. You're ashamed of me."

"Rowman."

"Your people never heard of a revolutionary midget, did they, that's what it is. They'd probably laugh and make me wear a gorilla suit."

"Hey, guys," Virgil said, practically hopping with excitement. "It's time to go."

"Rowman, you'd probably make a fortune back then, being from the Future and all, but—"

"Is it my suit? I got a green one at home. It'd match yours, except for that curly gold stuff."

"Rowman, look—"

Diego cleared his throat.

Virgil stopped hopping with excitement.

Rowman glared at him for interrupting his slow-building but inexorable guilt trip.

Belle stared at the wall.

Molly took a step back.

Satisfied that he had their attention, Diego met each of their gazes in turn except Belle's, walked to his chair, took his jacket from the back and slipped it on.

"Uh-oh," Molly said, backing away until she bumped into Virgil.

Diego picked his hat up from the coffee table, dusted the brim, and put it on.

"Oh god," Virgil said.

"What?" Rowman backed away fearfully. "What?"

Diego took out his Specials and made sure they were loaded, returned them to their holsters, and, after taking a long slow breath, pulled his spurs from their special pockets in his jacket and fastened them to his boots.

"Well . . . damnit," Molly said.

Diego adjusted his hat.

"There," she said to Barrows. "The hat thing."

"What does it mean?"

"We're doomed."

Then Diego stepped over to Belle, took her hand, and pulled her gently to her feet. Then he looked to the others and said, "I'm not going."

CHAPTER 4

Pandemonium, or as much of it as three people can create in a small space, took temporary control until Diego could stand no more, even though he knew that they had to let off a little steam now and then or go more loco than they already were. When he touched his hat again, they shut up; when he looked at Belle and saw her grinning, he frowned and her lips stopped grinning, but her eyes didn't; when he carefully buttoned his jacket so that the Diego Specials were hidden from view but easily accessible should the need arise, which it probably would knowing his luck, they dropped into the nearest chairs, couches, and floor and waited for the reason why, after all this time, and all his complaining about this Time not being his Time, he wasn't going to leave this Time to get back to his own Time now that the Time Thing was finally fixed.

"I don't belong here," he explained.

They waited.

He said nothing.

They waited.

He realized they hadn't the vaguest idea what he was talking about, but he wasn't sure he could put it into words they would understand, even though he didn't understand half the words they used anyway when they talked about things he didn't understand even if he knew all the words.

Belle cleared her throat.

Diego waited.

"It's the Book," she said to Virgil. "The one you told me about is the one that Bufoally uses for his trumped-up religion thing that Rowman and his people are fighting. So even if Diego leaves, he'll still be here."

"And I don't belong here," Diego repeated.

Rowman scowled; Molly rolled her eyes; Virgil stood, sat, stood, sat, stood and was yanked down by Molly, who used him as a brace to stand and say, "So you're going to . . ."

"Yep."

"And I suppose we're supposed to . . ."

"Hope so."

"And if we do, then you'll be ready to . . ."

"I'll pray for it."

"But if we don't make it, then . . ."

"Don't even think about it."

Her lips moved as she ran through the conversation just to be sure she knew what she'd said. Then: "I don't suppose you'd want to cut cards for it."

He almost smiled. "It's my living," he reminded her.

"Oh sure. When you're not killing someone, it's your living."

He nodded.

She considered, then whacked Virgil across the top of his bald pate.

"Hey!" he protested.

"Unreleased aggression and unfulfilled frustration," she told him. "If I hit *him*, he'll shoot me." Then she hit him again.

"Shoot her," Virgil said.

"Shut up," Diego said.

They gaped.

He strode across the car and opened the elaborate liquor cabinet, and took out a bottle and five glasses which he put on the dining table. Rowman immediately offered to serve, but Diego barely heard him—for inside the cabinet, lodged in the back, was a small glittering object he didn't dare believe his eyes was really there. And when he reached in and took it out, he still couldn't believe his eyes even though now it was right there in front of him for all the world and four other people to see.

"Damn," Molly muttered.

Virgil only smiled.

Diego handed the small glittering object to Rowman. "Can you handle this?"

The little man's eyes widened. "Golly! My! Yow! I haven't seen one of these since my granny died falling off a matrix tech slide in the jungle."

Diego didn't ask.

But Rowman allowed as how he understood the principle, and could, with a full glass, remember how to apply himself to making it work the way it was supposed to.

Diego poured.

And as night drifted slowly toward dawn, and the five people in the parlor car, three of whom were Time Travelers and two of whom were in the wrong Time even if they didn't know it, emptied the bottle and fell slowly into life-affirming and resource-renewing sleep, the slow and plaintive wailing slide of a harmonica filled the car, the train, and the Union Station train graveyard with notes slow enough and plaintive enough to make the Devil gnash his teeth.

CHAPTER 5

"You can stop now."

"But I'm just getting the hang of it."

"I'll hang you if you don't shut up and go to sleep."

"All right, but *he's* gonna be pissed."

"He's snoring, he won't miss it."

"You kind of like him, don't you?"

"Shut up, Rowman."

"Yes, ma'am, Miss Belle."

"Good *night*, Rowman."

"Oh! Good night, Miss Molly."

"Good night, Belle."

"Good night, Molly."

"Good night, Belle."

"Good night, Rowman."

"Good night, Rowman."

"Jesus, you scared me! Good night, Virgil."

"And good night—"

"Virgil."

"What?"

"Don't start. And Rowman, you little creep, get your hand off my—"

"Well, I never!"

"Virgil, wake Diego up, I want somebody shot."

PART V

Looking Kind of Pale,

Rider

CHAPTER 1

Plans were something Diego made when things weren't going to be as simple as meeting the bad guy at high noon or one o'clock in the middle of a deserted street with people ducking for cover all over the place; plans were something he had in order to live a long and relatively unpunctured life; plans were developed over a friendly game of cards, or a solitary drink at the bar, or in his room at night when he tried to sleep and discovered he was too wound up over the next day's job to do anything but think; plans were things that invariably went wrong because the bad guy hardly ever knew about the plans and so didn't do what he was supposed to which, in turn, usually endangered that long and relatively unpunctured life.

So when he woke up at what he assumed was just after dawn, since his body had been conditioned to wake up at that time for nearly a score of years, he decided it was about time to make a plan for retrieving that Book, so that the preacher's religion would be undercut and thus, if not delete, at least diminish Diego's role in the future of not only Nashville and Greater Tennessee, but, probably, what the continental United States had turned into.

The problem was, not knowing much about Nashville in this Time (or in his own Time, for that matter), and not knowing anything at all about the outlying areas of this bizarre place, tended to make making plans akin to wandering around the edge of a gorge blindfolded—sooner or later you'll fall into something, but more than likely you'll end up severely punctured, if not dead. Of course not having a plan at all pretty much amounted to the same thing, which then left him with two choices—either give up and go back home and the hell with the Future as he had come to know it, or get really nervous about going into this thing blind, or forget about it and go back to sleep since he couldn't do anything about it in the first place, which was a third choice that just occurred to him and was, all in all, about the most attractive one.

Going back to sleep, however, was easier thought then done. Molly and Belle had taken the beds, Virgil and Rowman were sprawled on the couches, and he had tried his chair, the floor in here, the floor in the Center of Operations Room, and even the outside platform under the dripping ceiling. Right now he was back in his chair, bare feet propped on a footstool he found in the storeroom, neck cramping all to hell, and his head aching as if he'd slept on a rock all night.

Maybe he just ought to make a plan and see what happened. A vague plan that would therefore by definition be as flexible as possible when real life, or the bad guy, didn't do what they were supposed to. Which put him right back to not having a plan at all, a situation not entirely unpleasant since, in the deep recesses of his mind, he could hear himself snoring, a sure sign he had finally fallen asleep, a condition he reveled in until someone gently shook his shoulder and suggested it was time for him to wake up.

He opened one eye.

Rowman stood in front of him, short, silvery, and smiling nervously.

He closed the eye.

Rowman touched him again.

He opened the eye and said, "What time is it?"

"Around noon."

A little startled that he'd slept so long despite the discomfort, he groaned and pushed himself stiffly to a sitting position, rubbed his eyes, pushed his fingers back through his hair and looked blearily around the car. "Where is everybody?"

"Miss Molly and Virgil are up there," and he pointed toward the maybe silver metal hatch to the Center of Operations Room, "and Miss Belle's in there." He pointed to the bathroom.

Diego rubbed his face hard to erase the last of the sleep, rubbed his neck and shoulders to ease the stiffness, looked at his bare feet still propped on the footstool, and said, "It's late. Shouldn't have let me sleep so long."

Rowman plopped onto the couch and sat Indian-style. "No hurry, Mr. Diego. We—"

"Just . . . Diego."

The midget nodded agreeably.

"Anybody been around outside?"

"Nope. It's been quiet as a tomb."

Diego wasn't happy with the image, but he was less pleased to hear that Bufoally, or McJay, or one of the cowgirls or white Indians hadn't been snooping around. It didn't make sense. One of the first rules of not getting killed was knowing where the people who were trying to kill you were. And he had no doubt that the preacher would try to kill him as soon as he could. He had to. The Hangin' Salvation Gospel didn't sound like the sort of religion that depended upon its prophet coming around unexpectedly every couple of hundred years to save people, thus tossing all his preachers out of a job.

He shook his head then. What in god's name could *be* in that Book that someone could base a religion on? Not that he wanted to read the stupid thing. He knew what his life had been like—Jesus, *is* like, you're not dead yet, you know—and although it had somehow spurred Virgil Lecotta into becoming the scientist he had, it certainly didn't have much to do with folks falling on their knees and praying not to get hanged. They did that anyway. Especially the ones that got caught.

"So," Rowman said.

Diego looked at him, blinked heavily, and yawned so widely his jaw popped.

"So."

Diego spotted a coffeepot on the dining table, and a cup. He poured, tasted, grimaced but figured it was better than nothing and too early for bourbon.

"So."

"Yes, Mr. Barrows?"

"The plan," Rowman said eagerly. "What's the plan?"

Another thing about plans is that, if you had someone working with you, which he seldom did, and you told them about the plan, they invariably found something wrong with it, made suggestions of their own, and pouted all the way to

Sunday when you told them to go to hell. He suspected the
little silver fella was just such a person.

"Don't rightly know yet."

Rowman nodded as if he understood the need for keeping
one's cards close to one's vest, especially when it had silver
threads running through it.

Diego put the cup on the floor, looked toward the alcove,
and said, "She gonna be in there the rest of the day?"

"Hold your horses!" Belle shouted.

Diego had forgotten about the thinness of the walls.

"And," she added, "it's a stupid plan!"

"Haven't got one yet," he answered, feeling rather foolish
talking to a wall.

"Exactly."

He frowned.

The door opened, and she stepped into the room, hair still
in its ponytail, shirtsleeves still pleated to a razor's edge,
jeans still too tight for any normal human being, not that he
was complaining, and her feet still bare.

He hated to admit it, but she looked wonderful.

"The way I see it is this," she began, but never had a
chance to finish.

Virgil stepped out of the Center of Operations Room and
announced that all was ready.

"What's ready?" Diego asked.

"You ready?" Belle asked Rowman.

"As I'll ever be, Miss Belle," was the somewhat strained
answer as the midget slid off the couch and hurried up the
aisle without looking back.

"What's ready?" Diego asked.

Belle took his arm, hauled him to his feet, and pushed him
gently toward the front. "Virgil and Rowman's been making
a few small changes up there. To the computer that runs this
Thing thing."

Diego's mouth went dry.

"Amazing stuff," Virgil said delightedly as he hustled them
all in. "Diego, you wouldn't believe how much things have
changed in computer science in only a couple of hundred
years."

"You told me they wouldn't. Much."

The tall hefty young bald man shrugged. "I was wrong." He turned to Barrows. "So, you ready to give it a shot?"

"Give what a shot?" Diego asked, then shook his head to fend off all the potential answers. Instead, he crossed his arms over his chest and leaned against the wall, and watched as Molly began flicking switches and turning dials on the left-hand wall while Rowman sat on one of those uncomfortable-looking stool things facing the windows that weren't really windows on the right-hand wall. Lots of the lights were on. Many of them winked and blared; the others just kind of sat there, waiting for something to do.

Belle stood beside him, her voice hushed. "He's going to Ride the Road."

Diego straightened. "He's going to what?"

"I just made a few temporary modifications, that's all," Virgil explained distractedly as he arranged a twelve-inch circular pad on the shelf in front of Barrows. "A tweak here, a few new chips and things there . . ." He grinned, laughed once to himself, and clapped. "God, if I could only take some of this stuff back with me."

"See, sugar," Belle said, "Rowman and I did a little shopping this morning, while you were sawing lumber."

Diego didn't want to hear it.

"That's kind of a primitive contraption your friends have there, but we managed."

He tried to swallow and couldn't; he tried to work up some spit, and couldn't.

"We figured, see, this was the quickest way to find out what we need to know. You know?"

That's when Diego spotted the colored wires sticking out of the metal wall, wires he was pretty sure ought not to be sticking out of the metal wall in the first place, even though he didn't understand the slightest thing about computers. And if those wires weren't where they belonged . . .

He felt Molly's gaze, and looked at her.

"Like he said, it's only temporary," she explained.

"What is?"

She lifted a shoulder. "I don't know. You know. Disconnecting the Chronical Accelerator, the Temporal Locator, the Stabilizing Chronometer Adjustor, and the brakes."

He sagged against the door. He had no idea what any of

that meant except the brakes, but he suspected that the overall idea was that whatever Riding the Road meant, it also meant they couldn't travel through Time at the same time. He felt cold. He felt warm. He began to feel angry that they would jeopardize their Pasts for a Present gimmick they really didn't understand any better than he did; but when the notion that he ought to shoot someone automatically rose to his tingling fingertips, he also realized that standing here without his guns, jacket, or boots on probably didn't leave him much menace to play around with.

He settled for a soft growling instead.

"Hey, don't worry!" Virgil said cheerily. "Once again, you're here while we make history."

"My life," Diego muttered, "is complete."

"Not quite," Belle said.

He looked at her.

She looked away and said, "Rowman, are you sure you can handle it?"

The midget's head had sprouted wires of its own, all of them attached to tiny round metal things stuck to the balder sections of his scalp, and to his greying temples. He kept his gaze on the screen directly in front of him when he said, "Fifty-four years old, day before yesterday, heck of a party too, and I haven't been lost yet."

"There's always a first time."

"Don't you worry, Miss Belle. This isn't like shine. I won't puddle."

"No," she said sourly. "You'll fry."

The midget laughed, massaged his shoulders, and after a confident wink to all in the room, he placed his palms on the pad. A deep breath, and he nodded to Virgil, who hesitated before reaching over to a large red switch beside the screen. He looked back, and Rowman nodded again. He threw the switch. The screen instantly filled with numbers racing top to bottom so fast it was impossible for any one of them to catch anything but eyestrain.

Barrows slumped a little, then suddenly snapped rigid, then slumped, sagged, swayed just a hair, and finally drew back to the normal position taken by a midget with colored wires glued to his head.

"Tell me," Diego said.

"He's Riding."

"Meaning?"

Belle gestured toward the screen. "I ... he's ... it's like ... he's ... it's ...—"

"The brain," Molly said as she swiveled around, "is just like a computer. It takes in information, processes it, and gives you answers. But it's a zillion times more powerful than any computer we can make. Ever. Even now. What he's doing is Riding the Road." She half-closed an eye. "The Road, as I get it, is the electronic link between everything electronic on the electronic grid that links everything that's electronic in the country. No. The world."

The numbers raced on.

Diego felt that headache stirring. "He's reading those numbers?"

"No," Belle said. "Those numbers represent bits of information. They're what *we* see; what *he* sees are actual pictures."

"But how can he know—"

"The brain can. When he's done looking, we'll bring him home and he'll tell us what he found."

"What's he looking for?"

A startlingly clear image of Zannylee and several of her mechanical snakes suddenly popped into view on the screen.

Molly leaned over and whacked Rowman across the back of the head.

The numbers returned.

"Bufoally," Belle said.

"Well, hell," Diego said, "I could've put on the rest of my clothes and gone outside. He'd've come along sooner or later."

"No," she said.

"Would so."

"Well, yes, he would, but—"

"So?"

"No."

"But you just said yes."

Belle put a hand on his arm. "Diego. Try to follow me here, sugar, okay? Rowman's looking for Bufoally's personal and very own private computer. What we here in Greater Tennessee call a mind twin. Twin, for short, no offense to

Rowman. Everybody's got one. We get paid with it, bank
with it, play games with it, read with it, stuff like that. We
figured the preacher'd use his twin to work out ways to keep
his people together, keep 'em from straying to the Church of
the Martian Consortium, or the Temple of the Pretty Soon
Now Lord, places like that."

Zannylee popped up again.

Molly whacked him again.

The numbers took their time getting back to business.

"That boy has a crush," Belle said, chuckling.

Fifty-four ain't a boy, Diego thought; and it's too damn old
to be doing what he's doing.

The headache surged, ebbed, settled down and opted for
acting threatening.

He did his best to think then, and in thinking said, "If he
can do that, why doesn't everybody know what everybody
else is doing?"

"Safeguards," Molly muttered as she stared at the Rider
and the screen.

"Guards," Belle said. "Real guards. On the Road. Monsters, walls, some damn mean dogs, whatever you can think
of to keep folks away. You make your own to keep nosy people from being nosy."

"Monsters?"

Belle pointed at the screen. "In there, Diego, all those
things Rowman's seeing are real. In the Rider's world. They
can hurt you, they can maim you, they can kill you if you get
caught." Her expression hardened. "Riding the Road is only
for experts. Military, mostly. We've had whole damn wars
fought in there. That's why it finally—" She shut up and
crossed her arms over her chest.

Diego grunted. "Illegal."

She nodded. "Very."

"The Law?"

"They Ride too."

Diego allowed as how this was all very interesting, what
little he understood of it, but he suggested that it was a lot
easier in the old, old days, when all you needed for a ride was
a horse that wouldn't take a notion to throw you. Besides, he
added, he already knew where Bufoally was going to be to-

night, so this was all very impressive and just as unnecessary.

Belle stared at him. "You know?"

"Yep."

"Where?"

"Some place called the Palatial Something Arena."

She looked at Molly, who paled and looked at Virgil, who was busy grinning like an idiot at the screen and Rowman until Molly leaned over and whacked him, told him what Diego had just said, and he paled.

"How?" Virgil asked. "You ... we ..."

"A man don't notice what's around him, son, he ain't gonna know what's behind him."

Molly jumped to her feet and pointed a trembling finger at him. "You said that!"

He nodded. "Yep."

"No."

"I did." He turned to Belle. "I did. Just now. Didn't I?"

But Belle had taken a step away from him, as if he'd suddenly sprouted horns, a tail, and a huge unfriendly shotgun.

It only took him a handful of seconds to understand what had happened. It had, in fact, happened before, and it was getting damn unnerving, hearing people say that he had said what he had just said, only they hadn't heard it, they'd read it.

"The Book."

The women nodded.

Virgil nodded.

Rowman nodded, and tendrils of spiraling smoke began to rise from the nodes attached to his temples.

"Damn," Belle said. "He's being attacked."

"My god." Virgil reached out to grab the wires, yanked his hands back and rubbed them helplessly on his uniform. "What do we do?"

"If you disconnect him while he's Riding, you'll leave him in there. His mind," she added for Diego's benefit, which was all right with him, he appreciated the gesture. "We can only hope he'll get away."

"He said something about the pad ..."

Belle nodded. "When the numbers turn green, shut it down."

They waited.

Rowman twitched.

The numbers turned red.

"Bellshit," Belle whispered.

The numbers turned blue.

"Bellshit?" Molly said.

The numbers turned white.

Belle sagged against Diego, who automatically put his arm around her shoulders, and just as automatically snapped it away.

The numbers turned green.

"Now!" Belle cried.

Virgil slapped the red switch by the screen.

Molly slapped at every switch she could find.

Belle ran over and pulled the midget's hands from the pad.

Diego said and did nothing, but he swore to himself that when he got home, he was going to blow up the first train he saw, on general principles.

They waited.

Rowman moaned softly.

Diego turned to leave, and paused when he heard the little man clear his throat.

"Well?" Molly and Virgil asked in unison but from different sides of the room.

"Rowman?" Belle said anxiously.

Rowman, his face bloodless and colorless and altogether looking like paste, stared at them all in mild confusion, then looked straight at Diego.

"What do you know?" Diego asked.

Rowman grinned. "I'm in love."

CHAPTER 2

The way it seemed to work was this:

The Reverend Bufoally's Annual Prayer Feast Fest and Hangin' Salvation Service was going to be held at the Palatial Ol' Opry Arena this evening, starting at about nine o'clock, at which time the Trail of the Poke for the coming fiscal year would be announced, new pokes would be branded in the Duck Pond, and those who had strayed would be taken to special meetings where they would be advised of their rites in accordance with the wishes of the Grand Poke, who tended to reveal himself once every zillion years to the assembled faithful.

This year, simultaneously with the Grand Poke's anticipated appearance, Bufoally was also going to announce the beginning of the Crusade for Truth, Justice, and the Cowpoke Way, the means by which he intended to legally or otherwise take over the Greater Tennessee Legislature which, as it turned out, governed most of the land mass east of the Mississippi, west of some of the Appalachians, and south of the Michigan State University Student Complex border. There was no doubt that he would succeed; the only question remaining to the rest of the continent concerned the time it would take before the Pokes and their shine-addicted minions had control of everything south of the North Pole and north of the South Pole, between the Pacific and Atlantic oceans, and all islands thereunto included.

A purely unthinkable—nay, even eldritch—situation.

The GT Revolutionaries had planned to disrupt the meeting, discredit the preacher, and have a few drinks on the house, which was why Rowman had been practicing with the gorilla suit, but that was before Bufoally had infiltrated the GTR with a few clever pokes in disguise who proceeded to disrupt the revolutionaries by sowing dissension in the ranks and half their clothes to the other half. While the GTR had a few tricks of its own on the table, getting them out of the sewn sleeves being impossible at the time, their failure to gain widespread popular support had severely crippled their efforts. It wasn't that their goals weren't the goals of every democratically inclined citizen on the continent; it was, simply, fear that prevented that popular uprising to which the GTR so aspired.

Previous Riding had gained Rowman the names of the traitors in his midst. Or rather, in the midst of the GTR, since he was presently in the TT.

This time it had also gotten him a good look at an off-duty Zannylee Stonewall, who, he suspected, was like many women who lived on the dark side of Nashville and other cities within GT—they were former cowgirl pokes who, having renounced the idiocies preached by the preacher, were shunned by society not because of their renunciations, but because the pokes were damn sore losers and managed to insure that no one, not even the Government, hired them.

At any rate, after falling head over silver heels with the statuesque snake charmer, he suddenly found himself in the middle of a burning, parched, lifeless, horizon-wide desert, being chased by several hundred bloodthirsty men on nine-legged horses. It was only because of his size, and the fact that those horses were having a hell of a time coordinating themselves, that he was able to break free of the Ride and return safely to the TT in order to tell the others what, it turned out, Diego had already read on the posters no one evidently paid any attention to while they were running for their lives from the lynch mob.

He also learned a third thing:

Before he was sidetracked by the snakes, he found the secret way Bufoally used to get into the Arena without being seen, thus enabling his followers to believe that he had, other than the chariot with the horns and choir, special appearance powers they'd best not mess around with if they didn't want unsightly stretched necks and a one-way ticket to the Eternal Underground Calaboose.

He planned on using that secret appearance method tonight,

when he arrived in the Arena before several thousand screaming pokes and acolyte pokes . . . with the Grand Poke himself.

"You," the midget elaborated, pointing unnecessarily but
dramatically at Diego, who was the only one in the room
dressed in gambler's clothes, except for the hat and boots and
jacket, which were in the parlor car.

"But I'm here."

"Yes. But you'll be there. Not the you you, of course.
You're here. But the other you. Tonight. To start the revolution. Not *my* revolution. Yours."

"But who's the other me?"

"Someone who looks like you, I guess."

"But who looks like me?"

"Aside from you?"

"Stands to reason."

"I don't know. That's when everything changed, and I had
to run."

"So he knows you know what he's planning."

"You know, I never thought of that."

"But maybe he doesn't know exactly who you are."

"Maybe not. But he had a Rider in there, or I wouldn't
have been caught. I suspect he knows."

"No. Bufoally doesn't know."

"But the Rider does."

"Yep. *He* knows."

"I guess that means . . . I think it means . . . are you telling
me that I'm going to have to go back in there and find out
who that Rider is who knows who I am and what I know?"

"If you don't, pardner, he's going to tell the preacher, and
there's no way we'll get within twenty miles of that Arena tonight so we can do what we have to do. And if we can't do
what we have to do, we might as well hang it up." He cleared
his throat. "In a manner of speaking."

"But he'll be waiting for me, you know."

"I know."

"I could . . . die."

"I wish it could be another way, little fella, but I can't see
it from here."

"Hey, look, seeing as how I'm going to be going for another Ride, from which I do not expect to return, would y'all

mind not calling me 'little fella'? Seems to me I'm old enough to be your father."

"But you're not."

"No, he isn't your father. He's *my* father!"

CHAPTER 3

All those who weren't facing the hatch that led into the parlor car immediately spun around to face the hatch leading into the parlor car. At the same time, Molly and someone else gasped, Belle and someone else muttered a fiercesome oath, and Diego reached for his guns. Which weren't there. They were in the parlor car.

So was the dark-haired cowgirl in the startling blue clothes and white fringed boots, who stood braced for action in the aisle by the Chinese screens, her fingers hovering and twitching over the curved, yellow-tasseled handles of her gleaming machetes. "Just say the word, Daddy, and I'll have you out of here in a second."

"Sara?"

"Can't help the mess, though. You know how it is."

"Sara!"

Barrows pushed through the others gathered at the open hatch and hurried up to the young woman now revealed to be his daughter, scowling and slapping her hands away from the quick-draw blades. "Stop that, child. What are you doing here?"

She leaned over and whispered loud enough for everyone to hear, "The meeting, remember?"

Rowman looked heavenward and slapped his thigh. "Fiddle. Forgot all about it."

"What meeting?" Virgil asked, following Rowman into the parlor car.

The cowgirl named Sara instantly went for her weapons,

but her father captured her hands in time and held them tightly. When she glared, he explained; when she frowned, he clarified; when she saw Diego as he left the Center of Operations Room, she yelped and tried to run away, only her father's firm grip keeping her from dragging him too far along the aisle before Virgil caught up and stopped them.

Unable to think of anything else to do, he loomed.

The cowgirl blanched, her eyes widened, and she dropped heavily onto one of the couches, Rowman right beside her, patting her hands gently and telling her that everything was all right, they were in the company of friends. When she looked at him for something more than mere explanation and clarification, he added the information about Bufoally's nefarious plan for this very evening.

"But Daddy, that one there's the one who shot Roy Dail in the Alley!"

"Between the eyes," Belle corrected.

"Darlin'," her father said, "that no-good white Indian was a gollydamn shiner, a mean son of a bitch, a bastard in all senses of that particularly archaic word, a drunk, and he smelled like three-day road kill. Besides, he was from Virginia."

Puzzled and astonished at the paternal outburst, Sara leaned away from him. "What's road kill?"

"I don't know. I heard it in a book once. It was awful. So was Roy."

Angrily she broke free of his grip. "Daddy, how can you say that? I . . . I almost loved that man."

"You're young. You'll get over it."

She considered the nugget of wisdom, polished it a little, shrugged, and turned her unfocused anger on the object of her temper. "And look at *him*, Daddy, look! Why, he's still dressed like . . . *you* know."

"That's because he is," Molly told her wearily as she dropped into the other couch.

Rowman nodded when his daughter looked to him for the rebuttal of such an obviously false premise; Virgil nodded when her gaze happened to drift past him on its way to Belle, who nudged Diego into his chair and dropped to the floor beside him. And nodded.

"Lordy!" Sara cried in ever-increasing confusion. "It's her too!"

Nods all around did not disperse her bewilderment, nor did Diego's pulling on his socks and boots-with-spurs make her sputtering gain any reasonable coherence. As she babbled to herself in a semi-audible and therefore non-recordable monologue, Rowman explained to the others that Sara, his only child by his fifth or sixth wife, was as she seemed to be—an undercover cowgirl member of the GTR, picked because of her beauty, brains, and bravery to infiltrate the Inner Trail and deliver to the revolution as much confidential material as she could, without getting caught and, it goes without saying, hanged. In point of painful fact, he admitted sadly, after Bufoally had infiltrated the GTR and the infiltrators had been finally uprooted and tossed aside, Sara was the only eyes and ears they had left in the Hangin' Salvation camp.

"So what were you doing here yesterday morning?" Molly wanted to know. "Get outta my town and all that crap."

Sara's babbling subsided. She blinked several times, set her chin, adjusted her fringed skirt, and told them all with her posture and timbre of her voice that she was once again in control. "It was an act. Y'all weren't supposed to be here, and Roy . . ." She glanced around the parlor car. "Matter of fact, this train isn't supposed to be here. What's it doing here, Daddy?"

"A long story," he said. "Right now, we have to hear Diego's plan for taking care of Bufoally tonight."

Sara puffed her cheeks, blew out, and fell against the back of the couch. "You're really him, huh?"

Resigned, Diego nodded.

"You going to kill him?"

He felt the immediate expectancy and tension that swiftly, and predictably, filled the car. He didn't much like that. It pretty much always happened, usually when some innocent towheaded and impossibly freckle-faced child asked him to please blow the head off the bad man who murdered his maw and paw and made his grandmaw hike twenty miles to the creek for water so the bad man could shave and have some tea.

And he always had the same answer:

"I'll stop him."

While shooting generally took up a great deal of his dealings with the bad guys, he knew it wasn't always the best way
to achieve the desired result, which, admittedly more often
than not, resulted in shooting them anyway. He preferred,
however, to stop them. Shooting did that, no question about it,
but sometimes it paid to have the bad guys, once stopped but
not shot or at least still breathing, be around to tell other bad
guys what had happened so the other bad guys wouldn't do
what the first bad guys did. The other bad guys, the clear im-
plication was, might not get off so lucky.

Sara grasped the concept instantly. "So what's the plan?"

Diego sat back, crossed his legs, and rested his chin in a
palm as he commenced a thoughtful walk through the first of
several steps in formulating a workable plan:

He had to consider his available resources, which included
in this particular instance two folks in godawful green union
suits, a cowgirl spy in a tasteless rhinestone cowgirl hat
mostly purple, a ponytailed hooker in bare feet, and a midget
spy who was also the father of the cowgirl spy.

He next had to consider the skills and/or natural advantages
of those resources, which included looming, traveling through
Time, spying, hooking, running fast, Riding—whatever the
hell that meant—wielding a mean butter knife, and compre-
hending the language a hell of a lot better than he did even
though they all spoke the same language.

Then he had to consider how he might put those skills
and/or natural advantages to best use.

Five minutes later he still had no earthly idea, and Belle
tactfully suggested they take a break for lunch. The others
stretched, yawned, massaged themselves in their stiff joints
and muscles, and agreed. Since, however, it would be dangerous for them all to venture back out into Nashville, Sara volunteered to make the trip alone to the nearest rapid ingestion
mart since she wasn't wanted by anyone, especially after
Diego had plugged Roy, and could walk freely among the pedestrian crowds. Being stopped by another cowgirl, or a white
Indian, would not, therefore, pose any harm.

After she left, grousing about the credit she would lose in
feeding all these people and how come, if they were so smart,
they didn't bring any money with them, Virgil wondered if it
wouldn't be wise for the rest of them to take a nap until Sara

returned, to muster their inner strength and be prepared for what would surely be a very long night.

Diego disagreed.

"But we have hours yet," Molly protested.

"Good. Fix the Thing then. We won't have hours, or even more than a couple of minutes, once we're done with the preacher."

"But—"

Diego gave her a familiar look.

Molly grabbed Virgil's hand. "C'mon, lunk, let's get it over with."

"Hope I remember how to do it," Virgil said as they walked away. Then he looked over his shoulder into the sudden cold silence and grinned. "Just a joke."

"You don't fix it," Diego told him flatly, "your lungs get a nice long rest."

Virgil laughed.

Molly whispered something to him.

"He's not?"

She pulled him away.

"You're kidding, he really isn't?"

They ducked hastily into the other room.

"Well," Rowman said, standing, stretching, and swaying a little. "I am definitely going to lie down." He waved away a stray whiff of smoke from his left temple. "That Riding isn't easy."

Diego said nothing as the little man flopped onto a bed.

Belle said nothing when the midget muttered himself to sleep, mumbling about having no strength left for a ninth wife, but those snakes sure were a temptation.

Diego stared at the tips of his boots.

Belle stared at her toes, pushed herself to her feet, and said, "Think I'll go into that storeroom, see if I can find something to wear."

Diego watched her leave.

He watched her peek around the corner.

"You want to give me a hand?"

He shook his head.

A brief scowl crossed her face before, inexplicably, she smiled and disappeared.

Diego shook his head and closed his eyes. That woman was

going to take some figuring before he'd be able to understand her strange behavior. Meanwhile, there was a plan to work on, a second plan to work on in case the first plan didn't work, and a third plan which didn't need much working because, as it usually did, it consisted primarily of getting the hell out of wherever he was when the first two plans didn't work.

Up until now, it had worked every time.

Trouble was, now, there was no place to run to.

That was about the time Sara returned to the train, dropped a large carton onto the coffee table, and announced, "Soup's on," and when he looked at the triangular bowl she passed him and saw nothing inside but what seemed to be week-old sludge floating around in month-old tar, he knew he was in even worse trouble.

He never could fight his best on an empty stomach. Which is what it would be whether he ate this stuff or not.

O Lord, he thought as he dared himself to take a small bite, or sip, or whatever you did with this alleged meal, the next time I am bored and desire some excitement, just send down the lightning bolt and get it over with.

And that's about the time he heard Virgil say, "Oops."

CHAPTER 4

"Don't *do* that, Virge!"

"Virgil."

"He'll have a cow, for god's sake."

"Molly, he really ought to lighten up, don't you think? A sense of humor would take him a long way."

"Sure, sure. Just hurry up, okay? I'm hungry, and the food's here."

"No problem. Just have to stuff this stuff back into that stuff back there, twist the modulator to . . . then move this back to . . . then turn on this here and set the calibrations . . .

would you mind getting into the Driver's seat for a minute, test the you-knows?"

"Then will we be done?"

"Absolutely."

"Sure?"

"Trust me."

"Okay. But I'm going to close my door and use the intercom."

"What for?"

"Because if you say 'oops' again, I want him to have a clear shot."

"Psst, Sara, could you come in here a minute?"

"Sure, what do you ... lady lady, those are surely the ugliest boots I ever did see."

"It's all they've got."

"Man, they look like Daddy in one of his gorilla suits."

"Never mind that. Listen, Rowman says he knows the secret way into the Arena."

"Yep."

"If he's talking about the Arena jungle, we've got big trouble."

"Oh no, you really think so? No. Can't be. I've been in there a hundred times, know every inch of it. There isn't a secret place there."

"Well, if it was a secret, you wouldn't know it, would you?"

"I think so."

"Oh? You and the reverend get close?"

"Spies gotta do what spies gotta do. I didn't, I got more pride than that, but I came damn close couple of times. Lady lady, without that white suit, he is one sorry hound dog. Crying all the time. Believe me, he ain't no preacher, and he ain't no friend of mine, no shit."

"Well—"

"Besides, you were one of them once, right? You ought to know."

"I never!"

"No, the jungle, lady lady. I mean, the jungle."

"Oh. Yes. Sure."

"Look, I know it's going to be hard going back there tonight. They spot you, you're a zombie. Don't worry. I don't wear these things to keep my skirt up, you know."

"Thanks, Sara."

"Don't mention it. Now why don't you let me put these to good use. Let me trim those . . . things a little. You try to run in them, you're gonna fall on your ass sure as rain used to fall from the sky."

"Will it hurt?"

"Trust me."

"Wake up, Rowman, the food's here."

"Yow. It feels like I haven't slept at all."

"You going to be okay?"

"Fine, Mr. . . . I mean, Diego. Fine."

"Then tell me about this jungle Arena thing you keep talking about."

"Well, let me see . . . as I recall, it used to be some kind of hostelry a hundred twenty, hundred thirty years ago. Had this what you call the conservatory or something inside it, lots of plants and things. The whole thing was close to twelve, thirteen miles square before the Bulgarians took over."

"The who?"

"Bulgarians. They the ones caused the Great Split thing, got us Greater Tennessee, places like that. Anyway, something happened, earthquake or something, half the place fell down, the jungle took over the parking lot and the rest is history."

"Your history, not my history."

"Suit yourself. Anyway, about ten years ago Bufoally bought the place up, dug an Arena where the hotel used to be, kept the jungle, started the Trail and the Hangin' Salvation Gospel. Lots of people go in there, Diego, and lots of them don't come out."

"Jungle can be used for cover."

"Yeah, I guess so."

"You found the secret way to the Arena."

"I guess I did."

"So we ambush that fella somewhere along the way to the Arena."

"Might work. Then what?"

"I get the Book, we get out, I get rid of the Book, and that preacher fella, he doesn't have anything to preach with but his own big mouth."

"Diego, there are copies, you know. Just like the Bible or something. Little things you strap to your wrist."

"Rowman, something like this, if you don't have the original, it ain't worth spit in a snowstorm."

"Well . . ."

"One more thing."

"What's that?"

"He don't have me."

CHAPTER 5

There was a time once when Diego and a small group of men were looking for a murderer and a horse thief just north of the Red River. They had tracked the man to a stretch of woodland just before sunset, and since the men were reputed to be experts with a rifle and a couple of bowie knives they kept in their saddlebags, they decided to make camp on the far bank of a shallow creek and go after the outlaws in the morning. It had almost been pleasant, sitting out there under the stars, listening to one fella strumming a beat-up old guitar, listening to three others cheat the hell out of each other at cards, watching another read poetry to his horse, and listening to the rest trade lies about their exploits in the outlaw-chasing game. But the hours until dawn were long, and by the time the time came, the guitar fella was drunk, the card players had beaten each other practically senseless, and the poetry reader had eloped; so Diego had crossed the creek on foot, strolled bold as a rattler into the outlaw camp and asked them how much trouble they wanted to avoid and how long they wanted to live. The horse thief chose a fair trial; the murderer chose to test Diego's speed, failed, and was left in a shallow grave to rehearse the speech he'd give his Maker, assuming he got that far.

Diego had a similar feeling now.

With the food gone and Barrows back in bed, hoping to sleep off the last of the smoke that kept teasing his temples, there wasn't much for the others to do but wander around, wander outside to check to see if Bufoally had sent his spies snooping through the station, sit down, stand up and wander around some more, bicker a little, then bicker a lot, then stomp off into their respective corners, or the outside, and pout.

He stood it as long as he could, patience being an extreme virtue and veritable life-saver in his particular profession; then he walked over to the couch where Molly was admiring Sara's work on Belle's newly fashionable boots, took Sara's arm and brought her out to the platform.

She quailed.

He smiled.

She paled and glanced fearfully through the door window which Molly, in her boredom, had cleaned.

"The Arena," he said.

She trembled.

"Little lady," he said, even though she was a good head taller than her father, "I don't expect we're going to walk there, right?"

A long second passed before comprehension nudged the apprehension from her eyes. "Right."

"You being the only one they aren't after, you think you could get us something big enough to get where we're going without getting stopped?"

She chewed thoughtfully on her lower lip. "I don't . . ." She brightened. "Yes! Yeah! I have a friend—"

"It'll be dark soon," he said. "Maybe you'd better get going."

She nodded, grinned, practically leapt off the platform, then hurried back up. "Look, I don't want y'all to think I don't like you or anything, but . . . being with those pokes all day, I have to admit, looking at you like this is kind of real spooky."

For the first time in days, Diego allowed himself a genuine

laugh. "Well, Sara, look at it this way—imagine how the preacher's going to feel."

It was her turn to laugh. "Sarashit," she said in pure malicious delight. "The man's going to sarashit." And she was gone, running across the gravel toward the exit.

"Sarashit?" Molly said at the door.

Diego turned. "You want to use that knife, you'd better find something to sharpen it on."

She opened her mouth, nodded, closed her mouth and hurried back, calling to Virgil to find her something to sharpen the stupid butter knife with. At the same time, Belle came through to the platform, and he began to feel as if he'd changed his suit for a conductor's uniform. But she didn't say anything. She just leaned on the railing and stared at the grimy dripping disgusting wall in front of her.

"Trouble?" he said.

"Hell, no," she said, idly sharpening her pleats on the rail. "Just that I'm probably going to die tonight, that's all."

"Don't think so."

"Why? You have a special deal with God or something?"

He bit the inside of his cheek. "Nope. But according to some folks around here, I am the Grand Poke. That must count for something."

She couldn't help it; she smiled, turned, and leaned back against the railing, the smile fading slowly. "I wonder what McJay is doing?"

"Weasels are good at sneaking. Probably been sneaking all day."

"But we didn't see him."

"If he's a good weasel, we wouldn't."

She shivered. "Do you think he heard?"

"Heard what?" Virgil asked from the doorway.

"McJay," Diego said.

Virgil shook his head. "I doubt it. The walls of this train were reinforced before I put the Time Thing in place. Just in case, you know? He could've been right outside the window and wouldn't have heard a word."

"Heard what?" Rowman asked, slipping past Virgil to stand beside Belle.

"McJay," she told him.

He scoffed. "That fool can't hear his own footsteps. You ever been to his Alley shop?"

She nodded.

"You ever see that stupid coat he's got, the one with the rocket ships all over it? Yow!"

Diego said nothing.

Belle was still uneasy. "Just the same, I'd feel better if I knew he hadn't heard anything."

"Heard what?" Molly asked, testing her newly lethalized knife by splitting hairs she pulled from her head.

"McJay," Virgil said.

"Which one is that?"

"The ferret guy."

"Oh. So, did he?"

"What?"

"Hear anything?"

"No," Diego said firmly.

Then Belle straightened. "Damn."

"What?" Diego said, not liking the tone, the word, or the expression on her face.

"The Buffalo Herd." She looked at him anxiously. "What if they set the Herd loose tonight? They're usually guards, but if Bufoally knows we're going to try something, he might just put them in the jungle. For us."

"Do you know that for certain?"

She shook her head.

He nodded, and spread his arms to herd them all back inside. "Then we don't fret about it. No use fretting about things you can't do anything about until they happen. Get grey too fast that way."

"He said that," Molly whispered to Virgil.

"I know."

"You going to tell him?"

"You want to tell him?"

They looked over their shoulders, and Diego smiled; rather, he parted his lips in a smiling movement and showed his teeth, but they knew right away it wasn't a real smile. Then he touched Rowman's shoulder and told him where his daughter had gone. The midget chastised himself for not thinking of it first, but assured Diego that his little Sara, for all that she looked like a wax dummy in that outfit, was good

at what she did; if she said she'd get them transportation, he
could count on it.

"Don't suppose it'd be a horse."

Rowman laughed.

Diego didn't think it was funny.

Nor did he think it funny an hour later, when Sara, red-
faced and panting and purple rhinestone hat askew, burst into
the parlor car and told them she had gotten what they needed,
but they'd better hurry up because she was double-parked
outside the station. They had maybe five, ten minutes before
the pearls started asking questions.

As Diego strapped on his guns and grabbed for his hat and
jacket, she also told them that the entire city was in a strange
mood. Bufoally's people had been spreading the word about
the Grand Poke's appearance this evening, and what with the
elections coming up and the economy going all to South
America after the Bulgarians pulled out and all the excitement
of the past couple of days, it seemed like most of Greater
Tennessee was going to be out at the Arena.

"It's getting ugly out there," she said. "Real ugly."

"Yow," Rowman said miserably. "And me without my gorilla suit."

"Thought you hated that thing," Molly said.

"I do, but it takes a punch or a brick real good."

Meanwhile, Virgil secured the Center of Operations Room,
cleaned up the mess they'd made eating the sludge, and found
himself a short metal bar in the storeroom which he tucked
into his boot; Belle, bereft of weaponry, swung her arms
around menacingly; Molly tested her knife on another hair;
and Rowman wondered aloud how he was going to find the
secret entrance to the Arena with all those Buffalo roaming
around.

Diego drew his left, or emergency, gun, and cocked the
hammer.

The resultant silence wasn't deafening, but it made his ears
ring a little.

"We go," he said.

They went.

Except for Belle, who blocked his way at the door.

He looked at her.

She looked at him.

He thought of the poetry reader and reckoned he definitely had the better deal.

She kissed him.

He kissed her back.

She whispered something in his ear.

He blushed.

She laughed.

He scowled.

She paled, but laughed anyway.

O Lord, he thought as he closed the parlor car door behind him, You reckon You could hurry that lightning bolt a bit?

And it disturbed him to realize that, to some of the people he was going to see tonight, he was actually talking to himself.

"Diego!" Belle called from the head of the engine. "Move it, cowboy! The flyer's waiting."

"Coming," he said, then stopped halfway down the steps. "Flyer? What the hell do you mean, flyer?"

PART VI

Two Mules for Sister,

Sara

CHAPTER 1

They left Union Station in a hurry, and Diego had no time to ask Belle what she had meant by a flyer, although suspicion made him look up automatically, to see if he could spot one of those car things in the upper lane or around the tower buildings.

Nothing was there.

Instead, he saw a boulevard oddly deserted for the time of day, which was long past sunset, and oddly dark. None of the yelling, shouting, practically screaming neon signs had been activated, the green streetlamps gave off only a dim glow, and a slow wind lifted pale dust into the air. A glance to the top of the rise showed him nothing; a look in the other direction showed him only the faint lights off in the distance, blinking in and out of the foglike dust.

The only sound was the quiet *ching* of his spurs.

"Daddy?" Sara whispered tensely.

Rowman shook his head; he didn't get it either.

Diego did.

It was the feel, the scent, the sound of a town waiting to explode.

He shifted his foot, and the soft ring of his spurs startled them. Sara beckoned, and hurried over to a squarish, lumpish, aerodynamically impossible pile of borrowed junk parked at the curb.

"Hurry," she said.

They needed no encouragement.

Diego had ridden in an automobile before and had lived, so he figured this wouldn't be so bad after all, even if those tires did look a little square, and the light coating of rust did make the vehicle look as if it had bled to death four days ago, and the six doors were stuck, and the seat in back—which he chose without asking permission—was cramped enough to allow him to study at close range the fascinating contours of his knees.

In the bench seat ahead were Molly, Virgil, and Belle; Sara took the driver's seat, and Rowman sat beside her—riding shotgun, he said, even though Diego didn't see one and knew that if the revolutionary had had one, he wouldn't have been able to use it anyway.

That part was all right.

It was even all right when Sara switched on the engine, several thousand muted bulbs lit up across the dashboard, and an upward spiraling whine exploded beneath him. Had the roof been any higher, he would have killed himself.

"Ready?" she called over the noise.

Various nods and grunts encouraged her to pull away from the curb and head south, the car lurching, swaying, and swinging as if it had had a little too much of whatever fueled it, its speed matching that of an ancient coyote hot on the trail of scrawny prey.

The ukeleles and harmonicas and a truly classical tambourine fell away gradually, replaced by much shorter, plain stone squares with square windows in them. There was no neon here, no sign of commerce, and litter of various indescribably futuristic kinds blew away from the car, clung to the high curbs, clustered around the foundations of heavily gated shops, and rose into clumsy parodies of dust devils. Occasionally a shiner stumbled out of a doorway. Once, a pearl hovered over an intersection, its white globes pulsing.

This, Diego thought, was more of a desert than the desert was.

He leaned forward as far as his knees would allow and tapped Belle's shoulder. "How far?"

She peered through the grime-streaked windshield. "A few miles." She shifted until she could look over the back of her seat, swaying a bit to the vehicle's vibration. "We have to get on the stripway and—"

He frowned.

"In the road," she said. "Strips? Match the ones under your

car? Program your trip? Don't have to steer?" She sighed. "God, how did you drive in your time?"

"Got in the saddle."

Molly giggled; Virgil hushed her.

Diego shifted to keep his spurs from puncturing his rump. "You drive?"

Belle raised an eyebrow in a shrug. "Just a little. I'm not very good at it, you want to know the truth. Too many dials and things, makes me nervous. That's why I use the strip as much as I can."

"Can't use the strip tonight," Sara called over the engine's whine.

Belle turned around. "Why not?"

"There."

Diego tried to see between head and shoulders and grime, and saw that the boulevard had risen onto a bridge beneath which was, he guessed, the stripway—a wide, fifteen-lane road that was at the moment packed shoulder to shoulder with vehicles. So were the lanes above it, and the lanes above them. And they were all heading in the same direction. A sneeze, he thought, would cause a hell of a crash.

"Damn," Sara said, and that's when the part Diego could deal with was replaced by the part he felt he could possibly deal with, given enough time, enough instructions, and the rest of that bourbon back in the parlor car.

The whine altered pitch, and the junk pile lifted off the ground.

When Belle looked at him questioningly, he shook his head, not wanting an explanation because he knew he wouldn't understand it, wouldn't like it if he did, and besides, her looking at him while, at the same time, he could see trees forming out of the darkness *below* the car, was doing things to his stomach that, previously, only a middle-age woman of his acquaintance had done one exhilarating evening back in Baton Rouge. This, however, was not exhilarating in any sense of the word as he knew it; this was about as close to terrified as he had ever been, including going through the Lincoln Tunnel in New York; but at least then, the damn car had stayed on its wheels.

Rowman muttered something to his daughter. She argued a

little, then nodded agreement, and the vehicle banked sharply to the right.

Diego closed his eyes.

Very.

Very.

Tightly.

So tightly, in fact, that he was beginning to enjoy the pain a little, and definitely getting a kick out of the fireworks display racing across the backs of his eyelids. Peeking was out of the question. All he knew was that, a couple of hundred years ago, give or take half a century, Virgil had told him about airplanes and, while Diego was certainly fascinated by the concept of riding in an umpteen-for-god's-sake-*ton* metal crate miles above the earth with no strings or reins, he had had no intention of ever trying one out.

"Why not?" Virgil had asked in a dull moment when they weren't getting shot at.

"What do you see from up there?" he'd asked in turn.

"I don't know. Fields. Cities. Clouds."

"Can see them from down here."

"Yes, but it's so . . . so wonderful! So different!"

"What's the point?"

"Well, you can get from coast to coast in less than six hours."

"What's the point?"

"Get your business done faster. Haven't you ever wanted to get to the bad guys quicker so you could get it over with?"

"I go that fast, son, I'll get there before I know what I'm doing. And that, in my line of work, gets me dead."

A condition he felt very close to at the moment, even when Belle reached over her seat and patted his knee reassuringly.

"Wow," Molly said breathlessly.

"Wish I could figure out how it's done," Virgil said. "We could make a fortune."

Diego felt the junk pile turn again, and the engine coughed and stopped whining.

He froze.

"Sarashit," Sara said.

The engine coughed and resumed whining.

"Lights," Rowman told her.

Diego, eyes closed and knees crushing his chest, felt the lights go out.

"Oh boy," Molly said nervously.

"Hold my hand," said Virgil.

"I am."

"No, you're not."

"Oh . . . my."

Despite the almost terror, Diego accepted the idea behind the idiotic turning out of the lights maneuver while they were still in the air with other cars also in the air that now couldn't see them and just might crash into them, sending them spiraling to their mangled deaths into the trees below. Sneaking up on something, usually the camp of those he wanted to chastise in one lethal form or other, seldom worked either in broad daylight, or at night with everyone carrying torches so the horses wouldn't step into prairie-dog dens or rattlesnake nests. In instances like that, the wisest thing was to leave the horses behind, take off your spurs, and walk.

Walk, he thought dreamily; what a wonderful idea.

Belle patted his knee again.

He acknowledged her attempt at comfort with a grunt, and when the junk pile lurched violently downward, he grabbed her hand and held on.

Very.

Very.

Tightly.

"Just a few minutes," she gasped.

To what? he wondered.

The junk pile stabilized, but its speed increased dramatically.

"Diego . . ."

He swallowed as he was pressed back into his seat and his knees further tried to squeeze between his ribs.

"Diego . . ."

So they really were about to die, after all. That explained the passion in the woman's voice, and the way she tried to grasp the hand grasping his. Although he still wasn't sure about her, it was, he conceded, a lot better than holding a horse's hoof.

The junk pile slowed, and banked again sharply.

"Damnit, Diego!"

Cautiously he opened one eye and saw Belle, half over the back of the seat, her face contorted in the oddest expression of desire he had ever seen outside Fort Worth. Until the soundless frantic movement of her lips suggested that desire had long since been supplanted by agony, due in no small part to the crushing of her fingers.

He opened his hand.

She pulled away, gulping for air.

He closed the eye again when he saw the dark trees rush toward the windshield.

"Seatbelts," Sara ordered.

Diego said, "What?"

And the junk pile stopped so quickly, the breath was crushed out of his lungs, his spurs tickled the upper backs of his thighs, and his hat flew off into the seat ahead.

Blessed silence.

Life-affirming darkness.

And Molly said, "Anyone got a cigarette?"

CHAPTER 2

When the door didn't open fast enough, Diego kicked it open, stumbled outside, stumbled to the back of the junk pile, and kicked it as hard as he could. Twice. Then he pushed his jacket away from his guns, put his hands on his hips, and glared over the vehicle's ungainly contours, trying to locate the proper place to put four or five slugs so that it would never, ever do that to him again. By that time, the others had joined him, seemingly none the worse for wear.

"Nice," Rowman told his daughter proudly. "How'd you know the clearing was here?"

"Lucky guess."

Diego's head swiveled slowly toward her, and if it hadn't been for Belle's hand on his arm, Molly's hand on his other arm, and Virgil taking a friendly step in front of the woman, he just might have changed the direction of his intentions.

"We have to hurry," Sara reminded them.

Diego, however, was not yet ready to test his legs. He used the adjustment period to note that they were definitely in a thickly forested area that might well be called a jungle by someone who had never been to one; the trees ranged from thin to incredibly fat, and rose to a hundred feet above him, branches interlaced, thick underbrush beneath, and vines winding around just about every trunk. That he could see all this, dimly, was due to an impossibly huge and round moon faintly tinted the same rust color as the junk pile. For a brief moment he remembered that people actually lived up there; he shook his head quickly. He was having a hard enough time with the people living down here. And if getting up there was anything like getting here in that junk pile, he reckoned the people up there didn't get back down here very often. If ever. Assuming they even wanted to.

"The plan?" Molly asked him.

"The secret entrance," he answered.

Rowman then gathered them around and quickly sketched how things worked just prior to the advent of Bufoally and the Grand Poke; his explanation was interrupted several times with clarifications, corrections, and further explanations by both Sara the spy and Belle the former cowgirl.

Diego listened to as much as he needed to.

The Palatial Ol' Opry Arena was, essentially, a vast amphitheater built deep into the ground on the spot where the previous hostelry had been until the Bulgarians blew it up with their raucous parties. It held ten thousand people. A ten-foot doubly reinforced partonium waylon wall formed the Arena's perimeter. The floor of the Arena was one hundred yards long and sixty yards wide, in the center of which was a permanent rectangular stage raised six feet above the ground. Embedded in the floor of this stage were ivory-and-diamond longhorn steer horns; suspended artistically twenty feet above the stage were redwood-and-emerald longhorn steer horns; on the north side of the stage was a small corral where the initiates were held for the branding ceremony that made them full-fledged pokes; on the south side was another corral for those who would not heed the Hangin' Salvation Gospel.

On the far south side of the Arena's lush grass floor were tables set up for the party after the ceremony; on the far north side of the lush grass floor were the scaffolds, nine nooses, no waiting.

The Reverend Hiram Bufoally did not enter the Arena with his devoted cowgirl retinue and choir ensemble until every seat had been filled.

When he did, it was in his longhorn chariot, which circled the Arena five times before settling on the stage, choir singing, trumpet blaring, stuff like that.

Obviously, they had to get to the preacher before he went into the Arena.

To that end, there was a path nearby that led to a small staging area just south of the partonium waylon wall. It was in the jungle itself, and used by the pokes and heathens who were to be part of the ceremonies. Sara called it controlled chaos; Belle suggested she was too generous. Whatever it was, those folks were watched over by the Buffalo Herd, and freelance pearls who didn't have anything better to do that night.

Molly studied the tangled growth around them. "How do they get those huge pearl cars in here?"

"They don't," Belle said. "They use smaller ones."

"Ah."

"That's right, Miss Molly," Rowman said. "Two- or three-pearl carriers. They're called mini—"

"Stop," Molly commanded.

The midget looked at her.

"Trust me," she said when Diego looked at her as well. "Just . . . trust me."

He shrugged, checked the moonlit sky just in case that lightning bolt had gotten lost, then motioned Sara to lead them into the jungle.

She did.

And single file they made their way along a rough narrow path strewn with rocks and roots, sharp-edged leaves slicing for their faces, strange birds crying and cawing at them as the darkness deepened as the foliage blocked all but the most powerful of the moon's reflective rays. One hundred yards into the wilderness, other strange sounds filtered toward them: the muted strains of organ and trumpet music, the muffled sound of hundreds of voices, the birds again, and rustling in the underbrush as invisible creatures patiently paced them.

"Man," Virgil whispered, "it's a jungle in here."

Diego, not being familiar with jungles, had to take his word for it as he brought up the end of the line. He stumbled several times, swatted at branches that tried to blind him, and hoped he'd be in one piece once they reached their destination. As it was, he hoped as he tripped again that he wouldn't have to run through the jungle. He'd break his damn neck. Then he thought he heard a rumbling, calling out his name, and when he turned he saw a shadow flit across the path.

He stopped, cocked his head, and listened.

But there was nothing but the birds and the invisible animals and the voices and the organ and the trumpet, and Belle hissing at him to stop gawking, they had a job to do, Greater Tennessee to save, didn't he remember?

He did; to his rapidly becoming eternal regret, he surely did.

Onward, then, and the noise of the crowd grew, and brilliant white light formed a fan-shaped cloud in the sky some distance away. Sara passed back word that they had less than a mile to go, so they had better start listening and watching for signs of the Herd.

The farther they walked, the warmer it became, until Diego's shirt threatened to permanently adhere itself to his back and chest. Unlike the desert, however, this was a heat that sapped his energy and made it difficult to breathe, and it wasn't long before everyone was panting, slowing, and finally stopping at a place where the path widened slightly.

"I'm going to lose twenty pounds," Molly complained. She tried to swipe her damp hair from her brow, growled, and clawed at it instead.

The noise now was clear, loud, and constant.

Rowman suggested that Sara go on ahead and reconnoiter the staging area. Not only was she dressed for it, but many of the regulars knew her, thus guaranteeing no suspicion be raised.

Diego didn't argue, but neither did he like it. He couldn't help remembering the trouble Barrows had had on the Ride, and after the street riot on the first night, he was positive that the preacher had something up his sleeve besides hair and warts. When the others gratefully sagged to the ground to rest, he prowled up and down the path, peering hard into the shifting shadows the brilliant light created, seeing things he knew were his imagination and wishing his imagination would knock it the hell off.

A hundred yards closer to the Arena, the crowd noise was such that it seemed close enough to touch, and as he glanced around he realized that the jungle had thinned considerably. He nodded. This wasn't a natural occurrence; security was easier with less trees and bushes to hide behind.

Rowman came up behind him then, deliberately making noise, which Diego appreciated since his fingers were just about twitching off his knuckles.

"Hard to believe," Diego said, nodding toward the light.

"People need it sometimes," the little man said.

"I know. But ... cowboys?"

By then, the others had joined them, and Molly told him how, in her Time, his Future but Rowman's Past, cowboys sang and rode gorgeous horses and had about seven thousand bullets in their guns. The depictions turned a little gritty after all, but still, with cities growing so fast, and the country fast shrinking, some people yearned for what they thought were the Good Old Days, which were, of course, not Diego's Good Old Days, but their Good Old Days.

"Looks like it kinda got out of hand," he said.

"It wasn't ...?" Belle's voice hinted at melancholy. "It wasn't like that?"

He didn't answer. Instead, he asked Rowman how much longer Sara would be.

"Yow, I don't know." He groaned.

"What?"

"Last time I heard, she was in charge of the mules. Damn, they might have grabbed her to work. She wouldn't dare say no."

"Mules?" Virgil asked, using his hands to describe long ears sticking above his head.

Rowman shook his head. "Workers. They clean the Arena, pick up the junk, pick up the clothes—"

"What clothes?"

The midget shrugged. "It gets kind of heated up in there once in a while. You know how it gets. You get those people roused and shouting and singing and hugging and ya-hooing and cowboying and hangin', sometimes they get a little carried away." He plucked at his silver uniform. "Got this only last month from Sara. You work it right, know a good mule, you don't ever have to spend a dime on shirts and shoes in your life. Saves the revolution a ton, that's for sure."

That's when they heard the first gunshot.

Diego drew as he spun toward the light.

Rowman yelped as he grabbed Diego's arm and spun him back again.

Diego snarled, freed himself, and spun around toward the light.

Belle yelped as she grabbed Diego's arm and spun him back again.

Diego snarled, kept his gun out, but didn't spin because his eyes were crossing a little, which was bad for his aim.

"No!" midget and hooker said.

"It's the Arena," Rowman added. "They always bring guns, to let the reverend know how worshipful and ready and willing they are."

"Blanks," Belle finished. "The Wild West, you see?"

He had. Often. But most of it was pretty dull most of the time. Not that they'd believe it, having met him. But they should have met a young San Antonio wheelwright he once knew; that man was so dull, you'd grow old and rot just watching him cross the street.

Nevertheless, when the sporadic gunshots continued, he had to force himself not to reach, not to draw, not to spin. It made his teeth ache. This whole mess was getting crazier by the minute, and him along with it. A preacher that used him to save and hang people and overthrow a government, gunshots you didn't draw to, white Indians, machete-packing cowgirls who wouldn't dare ride a horse, or a cow, in outfits like that, midgets in metal gorilla suits . . . he backed away, hands out to prove he was all right, and wished that junk pile was here because he damn sure needed something to kick about now.

When his vision finally cleared some and he was able to think straight, he looked at the others and assured them with a taut smile that he was ready to move on as soon as Sara returned, which had better be damn soon.

Then he looked at the ground.

Molly said, "What now?"

He looked up without raising his head. "You know what an earthquake is?"

Her eyes widened. "Oh . . . no."

He pointed at the earth. "Well, that ain't it."

They all felt it then, the faint rumbling and trembling, saw puffs of dust spurt weakly into the air, saw the leaves begin to sway, saw the vines begin to uncurl, and heard above all the other diverse elements of the holy racket . . . the thunder.

"You heard," he said flatly.

"Buffalo Herd," Belle whispered.

"I haven't made a sound," Virgil protested to Molly, who whacked his arm and made him yelp. "That doesn't count. The Buffalo heard?"

"Yes," Rowman said ominously.

"But how?"

"If you're big and stupid enough, you go in and ask for a uniform."

Diego looked immediately at Molly, who answered with a look, *if I say it, he'll believe it, and I'll regret it, so just ignore it, maybe he'll forget it.*

Diego did, because Belle grabbed his arm frantically, and pointed mutely behind him. He turned very carefully, and sighed when he spotted the large cloud of dust ghosting rapidly through the jungle, straight toward them.

CHAPTER 3

Indian wisdom had taught Diego that if you stood stock-still as a herd of buffalo stampeded toward you, they would, being the dumb and really smelly beasts that they are, go around you instead of over you because they'd think you were something that would hurt them if they hit you. The battered Indian who told him this swore it was true, although Diego thankfully never had a chance to prove him wrong.

From the groans, grunts, curses, and muffled sounds of collisions of this particular Herd, however, he knew that standing in the middle of the path was only going to get him trampled and ruin his new suit. So when someone yelled "Run!", he wasted no time charging between two large bush things and running as fast as the trees and other bush things would let him. That he was moving parallel to the charging Herd only meant that he would have to run faster, which he did, because he didn't want to run away from it since that would mean having to come back this way all over again, a trip that was not included in his as yet unformed plan.

Luckily, the shadows, the trees, and the bushes not only made it difficult for him to see, they also, with those artificial buffalo heads, made it practically impossible for the Herd to see, and he was able to slow down a little and get to the far side of the stampede with no more injury than a couple of scratches, and a thump on the knee when he didn't recognize a stump that popped into his way; he thought it was Rowman.

He leaned his back against a trunk then as the Herd thundered past, its individual components shouting futile instructions to each other, most of which seemed to consist of "Watch out for that damn tree!"

As soon as the last straggler thundered by, he moved swiftly to his left, angling as best he could toward the path. None of the others had made it with him, and he could only hope that the Herd hadn't done them any damage, although they'd have to be pretty thick to get in the way. It was hard to imagine that a man like Bufoally, clever and unscrupulous as he was, could have such a ridiculous contingent for a private army. Yet he had seen its effect on the streets—as with Virgil's looming, intimidation often worked far better than outright threats.

Which thought he held grimly when one of them stepped out from behind a large gnarled tree and said, "Hold it right there, heathen blasphemer. I got you surrounded." A second

Buffalo slipped away from the shadow of a tall bush, and a third angled in behind him.

Not, Diego realized, as dumb as he'd believed.

On the other hand, it was hard to be intimidated in the middle of a Tennessee jungle by three men who wore buffalo heads over their heads. They were tall, they were husky, and they didn't seem to carry any weapons. If they kept him caged, however, they just might beat him senseless.

He drew his right-hand gun. "Mind if I go through?"

The head Buffalo laughed hoarsely. "Jackass. You think those old things still work?"

Diego grazed him across the bulge of his left ankle bone. "Yep," he said as the man fell to his knees, screaming and kicking.

The other two charged belatedly, but Diego rounded on them, his revolver still smoking, and they stopped alive in their tracks. He waved his gun in the direction the rest of the Herd had taken. "Boys, time to find your friends."

They snarled, they pawed the ground with their phony hooves, but they picked up their partner and hurried off, false heads thrown back so they could avoid slamming their partner's ankle, head, and other exposed parts into the trees. It worked, most of the time. Diego, meanwhile, didn't give them a chance to regain their courage, or find it in the anger and humiliation they surely felt at the wounded man's expense—he ran on, keeping to the shadows as best he could when the shadows were really shadows and not trees that just looked like shadows. By the time he bulled through a long hedgelike length of brush and found the path again, he was almost cheerful; by the time he realized that he wasn't going to stumble upon the others without a little hard work, that cheer had begun to fade; by the time he figured that they were probably moving forward in hopes of running across him, he was growing fairly agitated, especially when he considered the possible fact that he was wrong.

But he moved on anyway.

Walking, this time, with a long bold stride.

The brilliant white light ahead blossoming as he neared it, becoming glaring, nearly erasing the jungle save for those trees closest to him.

The noise began to separate into its distinct parts, and he could make out some singing, though the words were unintelligible. It didn't matter. He had heard that kind of music before. Most of the time it was joyful and wonderful, and inspired a lot of genuine toe-tapping and handclapping and good feelings all around; there were other times, though, when the toe-tapping and handclapping moved on a notch, to mindless and fearsome ecstasy, the kind easily exploited by men like Reverend Bufoally.

It made him uneasy.

Soon, these would not be the sort of people you reasoned with, with or without a new suit and a gun.

Damn, he wished someone would catch up with him. He had no idea which end of the Arena was the south end; and if he couldn't find the south end, and quickly, he had no chance finding the secret entrance on his own.

Closer; and the white light began to concentrate its effect on the sky, burying the moon and killing the stars, and allowing a dark shadow to emerge at its base.

Closer still, and slower; and he recognized what could only be the wall around the Arena, perfectly flat on top but alternately bumpy and ragged across its unbroken surface.

Even closer; and he ducked into the trees when he saw figures moving around, most of them hurrying around the evidently circular structure to his left, while a handful hurried just as quickly to his right. The latter, as best he could tell, were white Indians and cowgirls. None had spotted him, and a check behind showed him no sign of the Herd returning.

And no sign of his friends.

He reached into an inside pocket for the leather strips he generally wrapped around his spurs when he was doing a little sneaking around, but when the music/noise/singing level rose to earache level, he changed his mind. An avalanche wouldn't have alerted these folks tonight.

As he kept to the protection the now sparse jungle offered, he followed the curve of the wall. Taking his time in spite of the urgency that made him want to run. No mistakes were allowed. Do something stupid now and he'd end up down in the Arena, in the holding pen for the hopeless. Though he couldn't help feel a tightness across his chest, he was grateful that he was at least in reasonably familiar country, what with the trees and underbrush and all. Slim comfort was better than no comfort at all.

He saw it then, and stopped, took off his hat, and rested a few seconds against a tree that seemed more vine than bark.

The staging area was a clearing not a hundred yards straight ahead. The only light came from the Arena's glow, and he could see several dozen people milling around. One last check in case Molly, or Virgil, or Belle, or Rowman had joined him, one last curse when they hadn't, and he began a tree-by-tree advance, one gun out, the other hand checking to be sure his knife was still where it was supposed to be and that the second gun was ready to draw if needed.

Sweat slicked across his face.

His boots began to feel leaden.

The figures became cowgirls standing around with their hands poised over their machetes while white Indians gathered at least two dozen ordinary-dressed civilians into a line, each member with his hands tied in front of him and tethered to the other by a rope tied around his waist. They looked terrified, and Diego shook his head to keep from grinding his teeth.

Another pause as the singing shrieked to an impassioned crescendo, and he made his way to the clearing's edge, just as a pot-bellied white Indian walked up to a cowgirl and said, "I need two mules for Sister, Sara."

"Well, she can damn well get 'em for herself," Sara Barrows snapped. "Can't you see I'm busy?"

The white Indian scratched his belly in puzzlement. "But you're just standing here."

Sara nodded meaningfully. "Right, Harvey. That's why you're an Indian and I'm a cowgirl."

Harvey conceded the point with a nod and moved on.

As soon as she was alone, Diego hissed at her.

She froze.

He hissed again.

She backed up slowly.

He waited until she was within arm's reach, and hissed at her to stop.

She stopped.

"Where's the entrance?" he whispered.

The line of heathens began to march toward the Arena.

"Diego?"

"The entrance!"

"Where's my father?"

"Who you talking to, Sara," Harvey asked suspiciously, tomahawk at the ready.

"I'm praying," she snapped.

"But you're not supposed to pray until you're inside."

She glared at him, and her left hand twitched over her machete. "Trust me, Harvey. I have a pretty good line to the Cowpoke."

"And so do we all," he answered piously.

The other cowgirls began to form a double line on the far side of the clearing, twittering, muttering, smoothing their skirts and setting their hats.

"You'd better get going, Sara," Harvey warned. "If you're late, the Reverend . . . well, you know."

She nodded, hesitated, but it was clear the conscientious idiot wasn't going to leave until she took her position.

Diego, however, didn't want her to take her position. So he stepped around the tree, whipped his arm around Harvey's neck, and dragged him back into the shadows and onto the ground. Harvey gaped when he saw the face above him, and sighed when the face smiled just before the hand Harvey didn't see clipped the boy's head lightly with the butt of the gun. It was an art. Too hard, and the skull had a tendency to crack and shatter and bleed all over the place; too light, and the victim was only momentarily dazed.

Diego was an artist.

The boy's lights went out.

Then Diego jumped to his feet, reached out, and grabbed Sara before she was able to move out from under the tree.

"They'll miss me!" she protested.

"I miss you more," he said. "The entrance."

Flustered, she stalled for a few seconds, took a look around the clearing, and pointed into the jungle. "Daddy said it was back that way."

"I know that. Where?"

"I don't know. It's a secret."

A sudden commotion behind them stopped him from doing

something dumb, like taking her by the throat; he used the distraction to check on the progress of the heathens and the cowgirls . . . and groaned.

"What?"

He pointed.

A group of Buffalo and white Indians had entered the staging area from the other side, and in their cackling midst were Molly, Virgil, and Rowman. They seemed to be all right, but Molly looked mad enough to chew nails and spit rust, and the men were slightly bedraggled.

Belle was nowhere in sight.

Sara opened her mouth to cry out to her father, but Diego stopped her with a hand, held her close and spoke quickly into her ear, earnestly when she struggled, angrily when she tried to stomp on his instep, furiously when she tried to gnaw her way through his palm. Eventually she calmed down long enough for him to release her, at which point he ordered her to get back in there, act like nothing had happened, and keep her eye on the new heathens now being tethered to the end of the line. If she saw a chance to free them, take it; if she didn't, she'd have to wait for his signal.

"What signal?"

"You'll know it when you see it."

"I thought I knew you when I saw you, but it wasn't you, it was you."

"Sara, you're wasting—"

"I thought I knew Daddy one time, too, but he was in that awful gorilla thing, and I didn't know him until I saw him get out. He looked awful, too."

"Sara, damnit—"

"So this signal—"

He put his hand back over her mouth, and stared long and hard at her startled face, thinking she must be a descendant of Virgil's; there couldn't be two unique people like that in anyone's history.

"Do as I say?"

She nodded.

He took the hand away, and laid it gently on her shoulder. "He'll be all right, little girl. You have my word."

Before she could respond, he spun around and hurried deeper into the jungle, trusting that she'd get her wits together

before it was too late. As for the signal, he'd figure that out
when he got to when he needed it.

Then he stopped.

The jungle had fallen silent.

No singing, no trumpets, no hysterical noise.

Damn, he thought, and hoped he wasn't too late.

PART VII

Swing Low,

Sweet Longhorn Chariot

CHAPTER 1

Sara Barrows strode nonchalantly into the staging area, skirt a-swinging and machete tassels a-swaying. She greeted those she knew with a curt nod and taut smile, shook her head when someone asked if she had seen Harvey, and planted herself next to the heathen line as the Heathen Wrangler up front checked his watch, and the Buffalo Herd dispersed to take its position inside the Arena. One of them, she noted, was limping pretty badly.

The line shuffled forward, and soon Molly stood right beside her.

"So what's the plan?" Molly whispered from the side of her mouth.

Sara keep her gaze straight ahead. "Have to wait for the signal."

"What signal?"

"I don't know."

Three men with shimmering air guitars and an atmospheric drum set minus the cymbals, hustled by, mumbling about union rules and time-and-a-half, and did anyone know the stupid words to "Happy Trails"?

"What do you mean, you don't know?" Virgil asked from the side of his mouth.

"He didn't tell me."

"Diego didn't tell you what the signal was?"

"Hush!" Sara looked around fearfully. "Don't use that name, you jerk. You want to get hanged before the thing even starts?"

Virgil hunched his shoulders in apology.

"What signal?" her father asked. He didn't have to use the side of his mouth. No one saw him down there anyway.

"I said, he didn't tell me."

"Then how will you know?"

"He said I'd know it when I saw it."

"Well, what is it?" Virgil asked.

"I. Don't. Know."

"But how will you know it when you see it if you don't know what it is?"

A portly Buffalo lumbered down the length of the line, checking the ropes to be sure there wouldn't be a heathen-inspired attempt to escape. He glared at Sara, Sara glared haughtily back, and shoved Virgil, hard.

"Hey!"

"Just don't give me any of that heathen lip, green man," she snarled. Then she whispered, "You just wait for my signal when I see his signal."

"Then what?" Molly asked.

"I don't know. Do something."

"Like what?"

The Buffalo returned, grunted, pawing, snarling, spitting, finally pushing his false head back and sighing. "Man," he said, "it's murder in this thing. I can't wait to be an Indian."

Sara cocked a saucy hip and smiled prettily at him. "Me neither, Eddie Ray Bob, if you know what I mean, and you ain't that dumb."

Eddie Ray Bob blushed and moved on.

Sara rolled her eyes and moved up to flank Molly. Suddenly she leaned back as if struck, uttered a particularly obscene curse that made her father gasp and wonder where he'd gone wrong, and grabbed Molly's arm.

Molly wasn't sure how to react, so she didn't. Not when Sara spat over her shoulder, not when Sara yanked a hank of her hair, and not when Sara drew one of her machetes and held it over her head.

"You say that again about the Poke, lady lady," Sara shouted, "and I'll string you up myself!"

A few cowgirls cheered; a few white Indians whooped.

Molly stared at the blade and swallowed.

"What did you say?" Sara yelled.

Molly moved her lips soundlessly.

The blade hissed down, twirled, thunked into its holster.

"That's better," Sara said. "Now keep your yap shut, maybe the Poke'll have mercy."

Molly nodded meekly.

Sara stomped away toward the head of the line.

"Jesus, Moll," Virgil whispered behind her. "What did you say?"

"Nothing," she whispered back.

"But—"

"Hush, Virgil."

"But—"

Rowman kicked him in the ankle. "Hush!"

Virgil yelped. "But—"

A trumpet blew—a single note that hung over the jungle like a shroud.

An organ played—a single note that lay under the trumpet's note like a corpse.

And the Heathen Wrangler bellowed, "Okay, you pokes, head 'em up, move 'em out!"

CHAPTER 2

Diego didn't much like hunting around in the semi-dark half blind and not knowing what he was looking for. It all smacked of futility, and didn't taste very good either. But he pressed on, fighting the sense of urgency that demanded he panic. The secret entrance had to be around here somewhere, and most likely there would be someone around to guard it so that it would remain, for those who didn't know it, a secret.

That's when he rounded a particularly fat and slimy tree and saw the chariot.

That's when he realized Rowman Barrows had gotten it wrong.

That's when he understood, as much as he understood any-

thing these days, that there wasn't a secret entrance at all, just
a secret landing place for the chariot to use to take off from
just before it soared into the Arena and scared the Hell out of
the waverers and heathen. It had probably been brought here
earlier in the day so that the traffic arriving at the Arena
wouldn't spot it flying to the Arena, thus spoiling the effect
of the Reverend Bufoally soaring into the Arena as if from his
own personal consultation with the Grand Poke.

That, he figured, made about as much sense as anything
else.

He made a quick and silent circuit around the clearing, discovered no guards, and wasn't surprised. There came a time
in the careers of men like this preacher, in Diego's experience
with men like this preacher, when they considered themselves
fairly invulnerable, too important to be physically attacked,
too powerful to be messed with. Which, also in his experience, is just about the time somebody blew their heads off.

The chariot shone, the oversize horns gleamed, and the
door on the left side was up and open. From where he stood,
he could also see deep grooves in the hood, which explained
how Bufoally could stand up there with the reins without slid-
ing off. He could see as well the line of darkly tinted windows which, from this distance, were impenetrable. Just as he
was about to take a chance, check to see how many were inside and what he could do to make sure they didn't stay inside, someone stepped outside.

It was him.

Diego blinked.

Black, flat-crown hat, ruffled shirt, silver-threaded vest,
long black coat, everything, right down to the pair of Diego
Specials on his hip.

The light cast a shadow over his face, and before Diego
could change his position to see who was him, Bufoally left
the chariot, his blinding white jacket slung carefree-like over
his arm.

"You know what to do?" the preacher said to the other
Diego in the manner of all leaders who wanted to make sure
their minions and stooges knew what to do.

"Yes, sir," the imposter answered smartly.

Bufoally ran a rhinestone comb through his hair. "You
don't mess up now, boy, you hear me?"

"No, sir, I sure won't."

The preacher slipped on his jacket, checked his reflection in the side of the chariot, and was pleased at what he saw. "All you got to do is stand there, wave them pistols around a little, look mean, you got it?"

"Yes, sir."

"Somebody tries to touch you, shoot 'em."

"With what? I don't have any bullets."

Diego smiled. Sometimes you kept falling off your damn horse even when it was standing still, munching grass, switching its tail at flies; and sometimes a cannonball won't budge you from the saddle.

He adjusted his hat, pushed back his coat, flexed his fingers, and stepped out of the jungle.

"Gentlemen," he said, "I'd be obliged if you'd put your hands up."

The impostor jumped, then laughed when he saw what he saw stepping out of the jungle.

Bufoally only shook his head and snorted. "Boy, you know what kind of serious trouble you're in, wearing clothes like that in a place like this with people like that filling my Arena?"

It occurred to Diego then that he hadn't yet worked out how he was going to convince the preacher that he was who the other Diego was supposed to be. He supposed it wouldn't be easy.

"Now look," Bufoally said, crocodile smile on his lightly flushed face, "you just tucker yourself back into the jungle like a good fella, we'll forget all about it. I got business tonight, and I don't have time for crazies."

The impostor took a stern step forward, hands poised above his guns. "You heard the Reverend, mister. Get your sorry ass out of here."

Diego smiled tightly. "You want to shoot me, you got to look at me."

The impostor shook his head.

The preacher smoothed his lapels and hair. "Time. I don't have time for this." He gave the impostor a light shove on the shoulder. "Just do something, anything. Damn, I knew I should have had a Buffalo here. But no," he said to the sky. "No. I said, Hiram, you got the Grand Poke here, you can't

have anybody around seeing what's what. No." He glared at
Diego. "Nope. I got to be the Lone Ranger, you know what
I mean?"

"No," said Diego without looking away from the impostor.

"Don't matter. Poke, for god's sake, do something."

"Look at me," Diego ordered quietly.

The impostor refused.

"Look."

The impostor turned his back and lifted his shoulders in a
sigh.

"What the hell's going on here?" Bufoally demanded. He
grabbed the impostor's arm and spun him around. "You're
getting good coin for this, and if we don't get moving, you're
gonna get a noose, too."

The impostor trembled.

Diego took a step closer. "Ferret," he said, "you sure do
make one lousy cowboy."

Bufoally gasped in a most unpreacherlike manner.

Ferret McJay didn't gasp. He just took off his hat, faced
Diego reluctantly, and twitched his nose nervously. "Don't
shoot, okay?"

Diego laughed. "Wouldn't think of it." He drew his gun.

Bufoally fell feebly against the side of the chariot. "McJay,
you know this . . . this blasphemer?"

McJay nodded miserably.

"Be damned," the preacher said.

Diego glanced toward the jungle's interior. "You reckon
you could do me a favor, McJay?"

"Oh yes," the man answered fervently. "Anything you
say."

"You reckon you could run like hell and not stop until the
trees do?"

"In a minute, sir, yes sir, I sure could."

Diego nodded. "You reckon you could take off my clothes
first?"

"What?" Bufoally said loudly.

"What?" McJay said, less loudly because it was clear he
knew he'd have to do it but felt that a protest, however token
it was, would at least salvage some of his ferret manliness.
Then he stripped to his rhinestone underwear, asked and received permission to please keep the boots on so his feet

wouldn't shred, and then, faster than a speeding bullet but with a lot more noise, he vanished from the clearing.

Bufoally, meanwhile, had managed to pull himself together, and when Diego approached him, Special still at the ready, he gave him his best professional smile.

"Son, that was pretty damn fine work, yes sir, it surely was. How'd you like a job?"

"Nope," Diego said. "I just want the Book."

The preacher frowned. "The Book? What ..." His eyes widened. "What?"

This was the part of the plan that Diego really didn't like. Especially when he really hadn't had one in the first place. He could, of course, force the preacher to fetch the Book from the chariot, or he could disable the preacher and get it himself, or he could shoot the preacher and get it himself, or he could ignore the preacher and get it himself. But that wouldn't solve the problem of ten thousand people sitting in that Arena, waiting for salvation and a couple of hangings.

They would still believe.

Some of them would, anyway; the others were there just for the hangings.

"Blasphemer," the preacher sputtered.

Diego felt a glimmer.

"Defiler of the Trail," the preacher whimpered as he sidled toward the chariot door.

Diego felt a hunch as he moved the Special just enough to stop the preacher from moving.

"Demeaner of the Way," was the whispered imprecation.

Diego smiled.

Yep, he thought; sometimes a cannonball just whizzes past your ear, blows up the other guy.

The trumpet blew.

The organ played.

In helpless panic, Bufoally looked toward the Arena. "I got to ... they're waiting ... I ..."

The notes faded.

Silence fell over the Greater Tennessee jungle clearing.

The only sound was the silver music of Diego's spurs as he

walked slowly, very slowly, toward the man cowering against his white chariot.

"Who are you?" the preacher asked, finally truly afraid for his life.

Diego stretched his arm and aimed the Special at a spot fairly equidistant between those two blue eyes.

Bufoally closed them.

"Look at me," Diego said.

Quietly.

Very quietly.

The preacher, lips quivering, hands quaking, did.

"You believe this stuff, don't you?"

The preacher, surprised, nodded solemnly.

Diego, almost to his surprise, believed him.

"You know you got some of it wrong."

The preacher swallowed, tried to speak, and failed.

"The life back then ... it wasn't easy, but it was pretty good when you knew where to look, and when to look for it."

Bufoally almost collapsed. "He said that!"

Diego sighed. "If he did, seems to me you forgot it."

The preacher's hands gestured vaguely, helplessly. "You don't understand, mister. Whoever you are. This Time isn't like that Time. It's rough now. Too many people, you have to be stern, you have to have discipline, or it all falls apart and we're back living in caves."

Diego stepped back, but he didn't lower the gun.

The preacher straightened, not safe but feeling safer. "The man in that Book, he knew how to deal with heathen and the baser elements of teeming humanity. He ... he, to use an archaic expression, cleaned their clocks. Dusted the floor with them. Cleaned house. Made them straighten up and fly right." He stood even straighter. "He made life safe for those who were in the right." His voice rose. "He brought the real truth to a harsh world that needed not just the law, but justice!" He raised his right fist. "He rode the lonely trail day and night, night and day, never a friend by his side, never a woman to comfort him, never a horse that stayed with him for more than one trip, riding the range in pursuit of those who would mock civilization, hunting down those who laughed at the very concept of a free society." He raised his other fist. *"He tried to save the world as he knew it to protect the women and children from fates worse than death!"*

Diego blinked.

The trumpet blew again.
The organ played again.

Bufoally's eyes narrowed, the clear blue not so clear or innocent anymore.

"You, sir, are a perversion, a sickness, a disgusting creature of the dark with those fancy guns and in those fancy boots and those fancy spurs and that fancy hat and that sissy shirt and that fancy vest."

Sometimes, Diego thought, that cannonball whizzing past your ear makes you kind of deaf, too.

"You, *sir,* are a foul and loathsome denizen of the den of thieves that the Grand Poke worked his whole entire life to eradicate and erase and get rid of and make disappear and . . . and . . ."

"Abolish," Diego offered.

The preacher nodded vigorously. "Yes! *Yes!* Abolish!"

Diego had reckoned that the man's sincerity in his belief would make it easier for Diego to show him, in a gentle and reasonable way, where the basic tenets of the Way had strayed from the real trail Bufoally claimed to follow.

He hadn't counted on the man being nuts.

This required a change in methods.

Unfortunately Bufoally used the hesitation to his advantage by ducking into the chariot, and before Diego could follow, the door hissed shut and he heard the unmistakable whine of the engine starting up.

Of course, he thought, sometimes you only think that cannonball missed you.

Damn.

The trumpet blew again, a little desperately.
The organ didn't bother.

The chariot began to rock and shimmer as the whine rose in pitch and volume.

Diego ran to the door, looked for a handle, a knob, any-

thing he could grab onto; there was nothing. He moved to the
front and glared through the windshield, only barely able to
see the white suit and white hair seated at the controls. He
stood back, took aim, and fired, but the bullet only bounced
off and plunked one of the trees. Frustrated, knowing his
friends were going to die if he didn't do something, he kicked
at the tires, shot at the tires, took out his knife and tried to
slash the tires.

Nothing worked.

Then he saw a blur of white through one of the side windows, and he hurried up, looked in, and saw that blur of white
blur toward the front where, when he moved to the front and
peered in while the engine rose in pitch and the chariot rose
an inch or two off the ground, he saw the white blur merge
with the blinding white of the preacher, and realized that the
white blur was Belle, and she was trying to stop Bufoally
from taking off.

Damn, he thought, and thought damn again when Bufoally
slammed a vicious elbow into her chest and knocked her to
the floor.

Diego pounded the chariot in rage.

Belle heard, looked, saw, gasped, and began to point frantically at the preacher.

He shook his head, trying to tell her that he was locked out
and his guns weren't any use and he'd kicked the hell out of
the thing but that hadn't worked either.

Trying to sit up, trying to get a breath, she pointed again at
the preacher, made a few hand signals, and finally got to her
hands and knees, pushed up, and grabbed the air in front of
her as if she were—but the preacher reached around the seat
and slammed her again.

Diego, however, knew what she wanted.

He didn't believe it.

Well, he believed it, but he didn't believe she would actually believe he would take about the only chance he had left
to stop Bufoally from completing his horrible plan of over-
throwing the government and putting in its place the life he
thought Diego had lived, give or take a few hangings.

The chariot began to rise.

Diego saw Belle writhing in agony on the floor.

He saw Bufoally reach for the central control with his right hand, and raise his left hand to him in a decidedly untheological benediction, the gist of which Diego thought pretty farfetched and disgusting.

He thought of Molly and Virgil and Rowman and Sara.

He thought that the boys back in Albuquerque weren't going to believe a word of it.

Then, as the chariot roared and the choir sang and the trumpet blew and the organ pealed, Diego said, "Oh, the hell with it," leapt onto the hood, set his boots firmly into the grooves, and grabbed the reins.

He closed his eyes.

The chariot rose slowly, dust billowing around it.

He opened his eyes and stared at the top of a sixty-foot tree.

He didn't dare scream, but he did dare a glance over his shoulder as the chariot bucked, swerved, hitched, finally leveled and shot at treetop level toward the Palatial Ol' Opry Arena.

He just about screamed then.

Belle was driving.

CHAPTER 3

Virgil Lecotta stood tall and proud at the back of the crowded corral at the south side of the longhorn stage. He was not about to be cowed by the Buffalo grunting and pawing down there on the grass, nor would he be intimidated by the white Indians dancing around a bonfire on the west side of the Arena, and he certainly wasn't going to be frightened by the thousands of pokes jammed into the seats in the bowl-shaped depression. He had lived a fairly decent life, had invented Time Travel, and had come face-to-face with his childhood hero. How many others could say the same?

Molly, on the other hand, made him nervous.

The reason she made him nervous was because she wasn't nervous. Unlike the two dozen others in the corral who were weeping and wailing and gnashing their teeth if they had any, she stood calmly beside him, studying the crowds, the performances, the Arena, all as if she expected to go home tonight and put it all down in her diary.

Rowman, however, just stood there, eyes downcast, hands folded in front of him, not saying a word, not looking up whenever his daughter managed to get close enough to call his name.

Virgil couldn't stand it. "Moll, what's the matter?"

She looked up at him and smiled. "Nothing."

"But aren't you scared?"

"Mollyshitless," she answered, proving that she had finally gotten the hang of some portion of futuristic patois.

At last he understood—she was pretending to be brave so the bad guys wouldn't have the satisfaction of seeing how terrified she was. It made him proud. It made him hug her. It made him look down at her waist and say, "Who cut the rope?"

She jabbed his ribs with an elbow.

He huffed, blinked, and realized with a start that nearly made him cry out that clever Sara had actually sliced through the connecting rope when she had pretended to be angry with Molly back in the staging area. For a moment he was angry with himself—he should have thought of it first. But since he didn't, there was no sense berating himself since all's well that ends well as long as they can get out of here without being hanged. He looked around, and grunted. Fat chance.

Then Molly coughed harshly, bent over, gagged, straightened, leaned against him and whispered, "Knife."

He leaned over and whispered, "I don't have a knife."

"I do."

He looked.

She did, clasped in her tied hands.

It was the butter knife, and the second Rowman spotted it, he tossed aside his resignation and stood stalwartly between them so that others couldn't see.

"They can still see us," Molly complained, checking the loam where the Buffalo roamed.

She and Virgil closed the gap between them.

The trumpet sounded, the organ pealed, and in the distance they could hear the angels singing.

"He's coming!" Sara whispered frantically as she walked by the stage, pretending to ensure that the heathen weren't about to attempt a desperate escape, which they were but not all of them.

Every movement within the Arena stopped.

The crowd hushed.

The lights went out.

"Yow, good golly, Miss Molly," Rowman said in a muffled voice. "I can't see a—"

"Watch it!" Virgil warned, his voice oddly high-pitched.

"Sorry."

"No sweat."

"Easy for y'all to say. You should be down here, it's murder."

Suddenly Virgil felt his hands part, and under the cover of darkness, he rubbed the circulation back into his wrists and fingers, waited until Molly and the midget had freed each other, then pulled them all into the back corner. Now all he needed was a plan to get out of the Arena without ten thousand people, the Buffalo Herd, and four or five score cowgirls and white Indians catching on that he and his friends were leaving.

It would be tough.

The choir sounded closer.

Tension climbed.

Ten thousand people stirred in their seats.

A red spotlight snapped on, perfectly illuminating the nine-noose scaffold at the north end.

The heathen whimpered softly, and many fell to their knees in not very silent prayer.

Then a circle of white light that appeared to have no source exploded in the sky, and the crowd sighed its pleasure at the sight of the Trail's white chariot slowly circling above them.

"Oh boy," Molly said.

Lower circled the chariot.

The crowd rose to its collective feet.

The choir quieted.

The chariot dropped lower, wobbling a little.

"He must be nervous," Rowman guessed. "The Grand Poke and all."

Sara came up to the stage. "Daddy."

"What?"

"Something's wrong."

The three looked down at her.

She pointed at the chariot, bobbing and weaving. "He never comes like that."

"Oh boy," Molly said.

Suddenly the chariot straightened, picked up speed, and zoomed low over the heads of the assembled faithful, banked sharply, and zoomed low over the heads of those on the stage.

Virgil's eyes widened. "Good lord! Look up there! In the sky!"

"It's a bird?" Sara gasped.

"Hell no, it's a plane," Rowman corrected.

"Oh boy," Molly said.

For there, very clearly standing not very steadily on the hood of the celestial white chariot was the man they called . . . Diego. Holding onto the reins for dear life with one hand, his hat with the other.

The chariot shot straight up.

The chariot leveled.

The chariot began to lower.

The speechless crowd knew what it saw, and began to applaud, a sound that started low and built into a fair approximation of a very large musket battle in which no survivors were permitted.

The chariot lowered, glowing in the dark.

The applause increased, now intermingled with cheers and hallelujahs and hosannas and yippie-ki-yas.

"Drunk with power," said Rowman disgustedly when the chariot began wobbling again.

"Daddy," Sara said urgently. "Come on, let's get out of here now, before the lights come back on."

"Hey, Sara," said Eddie Ray Bob. "Pretty impressive, huh?"

She looked at the Buffalo.

Virgil looked at the Buffalo, looked at Molly who nodded, and reached over the corral's top rail. By the time Eddie Ray Bob knew what was happening, he'd been lifted off the ground by his false buffalo head, popped squarely across the temple with Virgil's short metal pipe previously hidden in his boot, dropped back to the ground and kicked under the stage by a more than willing Sara. Virgil then vaulted the rail, put on the head, and reached out to catch Molly. Rowman slipped out under the bottom rail.

"Green buffalo," Molly said, looking Virgil over. "Amazing."

The chariot drew even with the suspended horns, and the crowd, hoarse and breathless, had to shut up for a minute.

The glow from the vehicle spread angelically over the stage, catching Virgil and the others out in the open.

They looked up.

Diego looked down.

The chariot landed with an audible thump.

The crowd said nothing.

Diego dropped the reins and jumped off the hood.

He was alone on the stage as far as the world was concerned, a tall man in a black suit, the ivory handles of his Specials glowing in the glow.

The crowd waited.

Molly, Virgil, and Sara waited.

The heathen in the heathen corral waited.

But they were all except Molly and Virgil puzzled by the sudden sweet sound of a sad harmonica wafting through the air. They didn't know why, but somehow, the music . . . fit.

The chariot door hissed out and up.

The crowd gasped.

Diego stiffened.

"Oh boy," Molly said, grabbed Virgil's arm and dragged him around to the stage's front corner, the others following, not sure what was wrong.

Then Rowman groaned, the harmonica faltered, and Sara choked back a sob.

CHAPTER 4

The Reverend Hiram Bufoally stepped out of the chariot, one arm across Belle's throat, holding her close to his chest. In his free hand he had one of those funny-looking things Diego had seen singe the hair off a rioter. It was pointed at Belle's temple.

"One move," the preacher said, all his teeth showing, "and she fries."

The preacher's voice carried across the Arena, amplified in some way Diego didn't understand. He also heard the crowd suck a breath in horror and confusion, however, and it only served to prove that the plan he had come up with while flying into the Arena was the only one that would work. Although, he admitted for the record in case the plan didn't work and he didn't make it out of here alive, making the plan wasn't the only thing he did while he flew; and calling that other thing silent screaming didn't do it any justice.

Diego didn't move.

Belle, her face red, her eyes pleading, her hands trying to pry the thick arm away from her throat, struggled, but weakly.

"You bastard," Bufoally said, voice dripping with venom so strong it burned holes in the stage. "You son of a bitch!"

Ten thousand people gasped.

"Do you have any idea what you've done?" the preacher asked, puffed with righteousness and a mean headache where Belle had kicked him.

Diego adjusted his hat.

"Oh boy," Molly said, and gestured to the others—*get ready to run, guys, hell's gonna break loose.*

Bufoally threw Belle to the stage floor and stamped one foot on her hip, his weapon still aimed in the general direction of her head. Then he gestured to the crowd. "Did you really think you could fool these good people? Did you really believe these wonderful folks would fall for your lies?"

Diego pushed back his coat.

Belle tried to make herself one with the floor.

Rowman regained his senses and took to the harmonica again, nodding when he saw Diego's shoulder grow just a little straighter and his hands just a little calmer, and, amazingly enough, his whole self just a little taller.

Spittle flew from the corners of Bufoally's mouth as he shook his head in pious condemnation.

The crowd began to grumble; the cowgirls began to toy with their tassels; the Buffalo began to form into their Herd; the white Indians didn't know what to do so they stuck with the cowgirls because the Buffalo in stampede didn't care who they ran over.

Diego flexed his fingers.

The preacher laughed his derision.

Diego lifted his head so the man could see his face.

The crowd saw it before the preacher did; the crowd couldn't believe it; half the crowd checked their wrist copies of the Book and still didn't believe it but there it was, right there in front of them, and the Book didn't lie.

When Bufoally, who was having a hell of a time keeping Belle down with one foot, finally sensed something wrong and turned his gaze from the crowd to the man in the black suit, he nearly sucked in half the air in Greater Tennessee. He hadn't really been paying all that much attention out there in the clearing, half the time swearing to himself at McJay for running away, the other half looking into the barrel of that damn gun.

He got a good look now.

Diego made sure of it.

"Touch those guns," Bufoally said, "and the girl gets it."

The harmonica played, sweet and sad, and just this side of angry.

The crowd, used to trumpets and organs, shifted uneasily. They didn't quite see the point of the preacher threatening what appeared to be the genuine Grand Poke, unless there was something in chapter nine they had missed.

Diego only looked at him.

Bufoally's lips twitched. "You drop those guns now, you hear me?"

Diego only looked at him.

"Herd," Bufoally called. "Herd, take this man!"

The Herd didn't move.

Bufoally scowled, and jabbed with his weapon. "Five seconds, boy, and she's dead."

And he kicked her in the small of the back.

"Four seconds," and he kicked her again.

The harmonica stopped.

Everything stopped.

"You know who I am?" was the question that filled the Arena.

Bufoally laughed madly. He kicked Belle a third time.

"Shit, boy, I don't care if you're the Second Coming."

"Wrong," was the answer that made every man, woman, and child hold their breath again.

CHAPTER 5

"They call me ... Diego."

CHAPTER 6

It happened so fast that history, when it was written, couldn't figure it out, even though there were over ten thousand witnesses and a bunch of Buffalo looking on.

Bufoally staggered back.
Belle crawled away.
Molly urged the others to get the hell on the stage.

Bufoally looked to his congregation and cried, "Blasphemer!", aimed, and fired twice at the heart of the man who wore the black suit.

Diego stepped aside.
He drew.
He only fired once.

The thousands of pokes, and a couple of the heathen who had been temporarily branded again, screamed their anguish, their hatred, their rage, and their fury, and rushed the stage, grabbing anything or anyone they could use as a weapon.

Diego scooped Belle into his arms and dove into the chariot, quickly followed by Molly, Virgil, Sara, and Rowman.

"Who can drive this thing?" he wanted to know.

"Me," Belle volunteered, face contorted with pain.

"Who can drive this thing?" Diego wanted to know.

Sara leapt into the driver's seat, scanned the dashboard, muttered something about cheapjack custom jobs, warned everyone to put on their seatbelts, and gunned the engine.

No one had time to put on their seatbelts, so they were all flung to the floor and pretty much plastered there while she took the chariot damn near straight up into the night, banking left, then right, then left again, then right again, then diving, then climbing, then banking left and leveling out before banking to the right not as sharply as the other times and leveling out a second time, flying for just enough time to allow the others to make sure they were still alive before she dove again, banked again, climbed, dove, and finally said, "There. I think that ought to do it."

With Belle firmly clasped in his arms, Diego found himself wedged into a small corner of the back, watching groggily as Molly helped Virgil into a seat, Rowman crawled into the passenger seat beside his daughter, and the towers of Nashville rushed dead at them through the windshield.

He didn't bother to close his eyes.

As he had trained himself to do in the dim, distant, and by

now probably unreachable Past, he simply waited for the inevitable to do whatever it had in mind; only then would he figure out what he had to do to make the inevitable not quite as inescapable. Meanwhile, he used his equally trained fingers to make sure Belle hadn't had any bones broken, and when she arched her back and winced, and a spot of blood appeared on her lips, he asked Molly for help.

Sirens wailed; the pearls had been alerted.

"Molly!"

"Not now," she said, gripping her armrests so tightly her elbows were locked.

"Belle's hurt."

"Diego, I—"

The chariot dove, climbed, and banked.

Diego helplessly brushed the hair from Belle's face and gently took the ponytail from her mouth. He saw they were flying through the city now, nearly at street level, and he did his best to cushion the woman he was awfully fond of against the turns and climbs and dives and rolls and whatever else Sara could think of to make his life miserable and avoid capture by the law. As it turned out, she had quite an imagination.

The sirens faded, but didn't disappear.

Sara leaned toward her father, who leaned toward his daughter, and their conversation lasted but a few seconds before Virgil suggested, at the top of his strained voice, that the chariot was too damn big to squeeze through that damn alley up there.

It was.

They didn't.

Diego still kept his eyes open, holding Belle against him, feeling her heart fluttering against his hand, swearing that if he hadn't already taken care of the man who had hurt her, he would spend the rest of his life hunting down the man who had hurt her. Which, when he thought about it when it was over, was the first time he had ever made a vow like that about a woman. But before he could mull that particular bit of revelation over, Sara warned them to hold on, they were landing, and as soon as they did, they had better get out because she and Rowman were going to take this baby to the underriver network and see how they could best use it in their struggle against the imperialistic forces aligned against them and the masses.

Diego figured that meant they were going to hit the ground soon, braced himself, and when they did, figured the lightning bolt couldn't have done much more damage.

"Hurry!" Rowman said.

The door opened.

"Hurry!"

Molly and Virgil did.

Diego did too, as best he could with Belle cradled in his arms. At the door, however, he handed her over to Virgil, and looked back at the cowgirl spy and the revolutionary.

"Diego," Rowman said, voice choked with emotion. "Golly."

Diego reached out and shook his hand, then Sara's. "Sometimes you lose friends before you get to know them." He smiled. "I'm real proud to know you."

He backed out with a sketched salute, and as the door closed, he heard Sara say, "He said that, Daddy! I read the Book. He really said that!"

And he grinned as the chariot rose straight up, hovered, and fled.

When his gaze reluctantly left the sky, and the dwindling white star flying on its side, for god's sake, he saw that he was in an alley that forked several yards up ahead. Molly and Virgil took the fork to the right, and he sprinted to catch up, just as they ducked into an alcove which turned out to be a recessed doorway which opened onto what he recognized instantly as the main level of Union Station.

He didn't stop to look around; the sirens were louder, and there were more, much more, of them.

They rushed down the steps and into the railroad graveyard, slipped and ran over the gravel bed to the TT, and practically fell into the parlor car.

Virgil placed Belle on one of the beds, opened the hatch, and said, "Molly, position! Diego, sit!"

Diego sat on the edge of the bed and held Belle's hand.

The TT began to vibrate.

Belle's eyelids fluttered open. "Where . . .?"

Diego told her.

She tried to sit up, cried out, and fell back. "But I can't!"

"No choice."

"What's the matter?" Virgil called. "Is she all right?"

"Yes," Diego told him. He smiled at Belle. "Miss Starr, it appears you're going for a trip."

She sighed, gripped his hand, licked her dry lips. "When? Their Time?"

He almost didn't answer. The enormity of it hit him like a slap with a wet towel.

"No," he finally answered. "They promised me ... they said they would take me home first."

She stared at the ceiling for a long, long time.

The vibration increased, not enough to be unpleasant, just enough to be felt.

"Molly, ready?"

"Ready!"

"Diego, ready?"

"How the hell should I know?"

Which, when he thought about it, was the truth. The last two times he had been here when the TT did whatever it did when it launched itself into Time, he had been unconscious, or close to it. This was, therefore and in its own morbid way, fascinating, and he looked around to see if anything changed when the train left its station.

Nothing did.

Belle tugged at his hand.

"Don't worry," he said. "This Thing does wonders for bad backs and busted ribs."

Her laugh ended in a racking cough. Then she said, "Between the eyes, huh."

He lifted a shoulder, not bothering to tell her that he'd been aiming for the preacher's gunhand. Trouble was, her lying on the stage getting kicked and crying like that kind of threw him off.

Then he heard Virgil mutter something, and he heard Molly shriek, "Say ... what?"

He closed his eyes.

"Diego?"

He opened his eyes, and Belle, smiled wanly. "I didn't quite ... what did he say?"

"Nothing." He stroked her hair. "Didn't say anything."

Molly stomped into the parlor car and glared at them, hands on her hips. "You are just *not* going to believe this."

"Oops," Belle whispered. "That's what he said. He said 'oops.' "

Diego stared at Molly until she paled and retreated into the Center of Operations Room. Then, without a word, he eased Belle over, took off his hat, jacket, gunbelt, and boots, and settled onto the bed beside her, his back and head propped against the wall.

"You got enough room?" he asked, folding his hands over his stomach, crossing his legs at the ankles.

"Yes, but—"

"Go to sleep."

"Sure, but—"

He reached up and rapped against the wall.

A minute or so later, after much whispering and moving about, Virgil poked his head timidly around the hatch. "You want something?"

"Yep. Wake me when we get there."

"Sure."

"Wherever it is."

"Sure thing."

Diego closed his eyes.

Diego opened one eye; Virgil was still there.

"Oops?" he said.

Virgil sighed.

And nodded.

Diego closed the eye again, felt Belle take one of his hands and hold it, and decided that whatever Virgil had done wrong this time, it couldn't be worse than what he had done last time. They could have ended up on the Moon, and they hadn't; they could have ended up in the middle of an ocean, and they hadn't; they could have ended up back where they'd started from, and they hadn't. So all he had to do was be patient. Wait. Figure out a way he was going to get Belle better, and then figure out what the hell he'd do then.

Thus comforted and reassured, he let himself drift to the Time Thing's gentle vibrations, and when he was sure Belle had fallen asleep, he eased off the mattress, picked up his jacket and walked quietly to the back door.

From an inside pocket he took out the Book—a small

thing, covered with some sort of clear glassy material studded with rhinestones, some of which weren't even purple.

His name was on the cover.

Well, he thought to his distorted reflection in the once again Time-grimed window, you going to peek or not? The preacher's gone, without this that Poke and Trail and Way stuff is gone, who's gonna know?

It was tempting.

But not all that tempting.

From what Virgil and Molly had told him, half of what was in there was wrong, and he wasn't sure if he wanted to know if the half that was right was really right. Especially the ending. It would kind of take the edge off things if he knew that, might get sloppy, might get careless, and someone'd have to write another damn book to straighten things out.

He shuddered and, before he could change his mind, he opened the door just wide enough for his right hand to fling the book that was no longer the Book out into the Time Void fog that damn near froze his fingers off before he yanked them back and slammed the door again.

He stood there for a long time, shook his head, and finally grinned as he made his way back to the bed, lay down, and closed his eyes.

Drifted, thought about what in the name of heaven he was going to do about Belle when they got where they were going and he sincerely hoped it wasn't back to New York, fell into a light doze, snapped out of the light doze and did his best not to go for his guns when he heard Molly say, "Where? *Where?* You've got to be kidding."

Yep, Diego thought; story of my life.